ADOPTED

ROBERT OBERLE

PAGE PUBLISHING
Conneaut Lake, PA

First originally published by Page Publishing 2023

ISBN 978-1-6624-8597-8 (pbk)
ISBN 978-1-6624-8598-5 (digital)

Printed in the United States of America

I want to bring you an interesting story that is enjoyable to read and has some worthwhile things to take with you.

Robert Oberle

PROLOGUE

It was a clear, beautiful, springlike morning as the magnificent liner cruised toward Bermuda. The sea was calm, almost glasslike, with a soft breeze and several white puffy clouds dotting the sky. The gentle roll of the ship was almost unnoticeable, even to the weakest occasional cruise passenger. The perfect conditions were better than Emma had hoped for, as she took her first morning stroll along A deck before heading into the first-class restaurant known as The Admiral's Cove for a light breakfast. This was a great way to get away and really relax for a change, Emma told herself. She looked up over the starboard and saw a flock of gulls heading back to the mainland, a beautiful sight, for sure. She turned off the promenade and walked through an open corridor to the entrance of the restaurant and went inside. It was already somewhat crowded. She sat down at the first window table and waited a few moments for a waiter. She really felt relaxed; first time in years, she told herself.

The patrons seated there were mostly well dressed, sixty-something, successful-looking people; some were couples while others were not. She noticed that over half of them were women, perhaps considerably more than half, she thought.

"Good morning. I'm Carlos, I'll be your server. What can I get for you this beautiful morning?" the young Spanish-looking man asked.

Emma paused and noticed a buffet set up across the room. "I'll just have coffee and then maybe help myself over there," she said, pointing toward her new discovery.

The waiter smiled. "Coffee, just for you, coming pronto," he said, and then turned and left.

The room was beginning to fill at a faster rate. Emma took a moment before getting up. She could see that many of the single women seemed a bit jittery—no, more like nervous, being alone and yet out in public at the same time. That probably explained why she felt a bit off-center herself, she thought. She rose from the table and slowly made her way toward the great food display. She cautiously glanced from side to side, almost expecting to recognize someone, but no one was there whom she knew.

The line was short at the buffet. Emma took a deep breath and told herself to just relax, that this was fun, a great adventure, and, who knows, maybe even a mister right.

"Emma. Emma Molloy. Is that you?" a woman's voice asked.

Emma turned from the display and faced her and smiled politely, almost thinking she recognized her.

"Emma. It is you," the lady joyfully said. "Why, I'd recognize you anywhere," the woman continued. Emma was still having trouble. She just couldn't place her. "It's me, it's me, Susan Daniels, you remember? St. Rita's school, Sister Veronica von Whack-O, fifth through eighth grade. It's me. And you… you look…you look great," Susan exclaimed.

For Emma, it was starting to come back. Her polite smile turned to a smile of warming endearment. "Yes, Susan… Susan, it's you. I know you. You and I, St. Rita's, yes, I know you. How are you?" Emma asked, throwing her arms around her shoulders and giving her a warm hug. "Are you with anyone?" Emma asked, hoping the answer would be no.

Susan looked fondly at her old friend. "I'm here with you," she parried back.

"Then come, let's fill up right here together and go back to my table."

"We've got some catching up to do," Susan eagerly interrupted. They both laughed a small laugh and made their way across the seemingly unending food selections, and then walked over to Emma's table to sit down. Carlos was standing there.

"Let me get these chairs for you," he said, while taking their plates and seating them. Then he poured Emma's coffee. "And coffee for the lady?" he asked Susan. She nodded at him, and he turned and left.

"Emma," Susan started to say as a small tear formed just under her left eye. "Emma, I can't even begin to tell you how happy I am to see you. After all these years, to think about it, here…out here in the middle of nowhere, and there you are right before my very eyes, and it's really you," Susan said in a loving fashion.

Emma also felt very happy. "Susan, tell me, whatever happened to Barbara? Barbara, oh, I'll get her last name, give me a minute… Barbara McCloskey. You remember? Barbara 'The Gold Digger' McCloskey. I remember we used to call her that because she was always bragging that she could get any man she wanted but would only settle for one with tons of money. I hope she's all right. You've sometimes got to be careful for what you wish for." Susan smiled while she nodded at her old friend.

The waiter came back to the table and poured her coffee. "I'll be nearby if you care for anything else," he said and then left them.

"Susan, don't let your food get cold," Emma said. They both started eating, and then Susan suddenly stopped; she couldn't contain herself.

"Emma... Emma, you didn't know about McCloskey? She entered the sisters of Saint Joseph and became a nun. I think it was after her divorce. Well, at least that's what I heard, anyway."

"Who was she married to?" Emma asked her.

Susan laughed. "It was in the local paper. It seems that many years ago, she had been having an affair with that judge, oh, what's his name... Judge Wolman, I think. Who knows? But anyhow, a few years go by, and this judge tosses Barbara for a newer model. He tried keeping it out of the news, but McCloskey made sure she got it in, and boy, did she ever get it in. She told a reporter that her ex, the judge, had ties to the mob. So what happens next? They put a contract out on her right after the judge mysteriously turns up in the East River. She got tipped about the contract on her, and then the story goes McCloskey got depressed, started drinking, and saw the shrink. The usual, right?"

"Right," Emma answered, anxiously caught up in the story.

"But that didn't last long because from there, she felt too threatened, so she hid in the convent," Susan continued.

"That's about as safe a place as any, I suppose," Emma responded through a laugh.

Susan was laughing too. "You're right, Emma. You'd have to be a lot bigger than Barbara for them to take you out when you're in a convent," Susan quipped.

Emma looked a little more serious. "And what about you, Susan? Tell me about you," Emma prodded.

"Well, I'm enjoying this breakfast very much. The food is really good here, the company exceptional, and there may be one or two good-looking men in the room with us here today."

"Very funny," Emma replied. "I'll start over. Susan, Ms. or Mrs. Susan, how has life been treating you? Has it been kind?" Emma asked with a slight trepidation.

Susan looked down at her plate and raised her fork to her mouth and slowly began to chew. She thought about some of the things she had heard about Emma and knew that inevitably this line of questioning would lead to that. She didn't want to pry into Emma's life too much, but she also knew she would be there for her, if needed, as a friend.

"We sure had some good times together, Emma, back in the day," Susan evasively answered. "I really tried to keep up with you in track and other things as well. I thought I had you beat in English, I mean writing short stories and essays and things, but who went on to become the novelist? And the answer is Emma. You did. Now, please, don't get me wrong. I'm not the least bit jealous. I'm truly happy for you, I always have been. Don't think I haven't enjoyed dropping your name as my friend at a cocktail party or two because I have. I admit it, I'm no saint," Susan confessed.

Emma smiled at her. She could see that Susan was being sincere, that she was a true friend. It was just like all those years hadn't taken place, for they certainly hadn't come between them. Emma took a deep breath and went back to eating.

"Anything I can get for you?" Carlos asked them.

"We could use a little more coffee," Emma told him, and then she looked out at the room and saw one or two men who didn't look too bad, kind of nice, she thought. Carlos returned and filled them both up and left.

"Emma, I'll be honest with you. After Jim died three years ago, things were tough at first. I was lonely, a widow in my sixties, no kids, no career, and no prospects for any of the above. The money was okay. Jim left me well off, so that's not a problem. The problem is just getting up in the morning and trying to figure out what to do next. I suppose I'm not the only one. I'm not complaining, I mean I'm not complaining too much, am I?" she asked.

Emma looked at her with compassion. "You really were better than me at track," she playfully answered. "And besides, you were faster, so that made you better, only sometimes I was faster, but you were still better. I think that's how it works. But all kidding aside, I'm sorry about Jim. I didn't know you were married. I'm sorry for that too. It must be that life comes along and swallows up all your time, and before you know it, you're done, cooked, whatever, and you missed out on some really good things…good things that matter. Anyway, I feel that way, Susan. I really feel that way right now, but I suppose I'm not going to let it take me down just because a lot of things happened to me, especially things you never read about, things you never knew about. I don't want to burden you with any of my problems, so let's just leave it at that. Besides, we've got a cruise to get on with here, don't we?" Emma said, getting up from the table.

"Emma, I want you to promise me that you'll never use that word burden to me again," Susan scolded, as she also rose to her feet and followed Emma across the floor out of the restaurant and onto A deck. "Let's sit over there," Susan said, pointing to two unoccupied lounge chairs that were off by themselves. "Tell me about some of those things you were mentioning inside, Emma. Please feel free. We've got five more days and plenty of ocean ahead of us, so take your time because we've both got plenty of it," Susan encouraged.

Emma laughed a little. "Thank you, Susan," she slowly answered.

"That's what friends are for," Susan replied.

"Well, okay, you asked for it, so here it comes. I grew up in Flushing, New York, in the 1960s. My father's name was Tom, my mother's name was Pat, Patricia, really, but you know that. You knew them."

"We can move past the small talk, Emma. Yes, I knew them. I, at least, knew your mother. I think I might have met you father once when I was over there, but your mother, yes, definitely. She was a wonderful woman," Susan said, taking hold of her old friend's hand.

Emma took a deep breath and looked up toward the blue sky. She searched inside her purse for her sunglasses and put them on.

"You left out your sister," Susan interjected. "You left out Elizabeth. I remember her as if it were yesterday."

Emma recoiled. "Yes, you're right, Susan. Elizabeth," Emma slowly responded.

"Tell me about her," Susan nudged. "Is she all right? Where is she?" Emma began to frown at her. "I can take a hint, I'm sorry, Emma. Please, go on with your story, start from the beginning. I'm sorry," Susan pleaded as she, too, put on her sunglasses.

Emma sighed and then looked her straight in the eye and smiled, at first thinking to herself it really didn't matter at this stage of the game while keeping the smile plastered to her face. But then suddenly, something inside her made her hesitate, made her clutch, and she instinctively felt the over-powering need to hold back by changing to a safer topic as the distant, painful, memories began to well up inside.

"Elizabeth...she's fine," Emma nervously told her, not wanting to go on any further. But then luck broke her way. Susan's expression changed.

"Oh, I forgot, I'm sorry, Emma. I'm already late for my hairdresser's appointment," Susan said, glancing at her watch and then quickly rising to her feet. Emma felt extremely relieved and was careful not to say anything that would cause her to stay. "Can we get together later?" Susan asked, removing her glasses.

"Certainly, how about dinner?"

"Tonight?" Susan anxiously interrupted.

"Okay, tonight, say, seven, at our breakfast table so we'll both know where to go," Emma replied, trying to put a little humor on it.

"Okay, Emma, seven it is," Susan confirmed and then she turned and walked briskly away, back along the deck they had just both come up on. Emma finally relaxed. She lay back in the big deck chair and began drifting off into her own little world, seeing her sister, Elizabeth, and both remembering and imagining how life had really been. Some of the things she knew about, and others she had only heard about, but it didn't matter because they all came together in her mind. And all the while, as she lay back in that beautiful setting, Emma kept wondering how much she really wanted to tell her old friend, or anyone else, for that matter.

Then Emma's mind focused back on the latest argument she had had with her sister, Elizabeth. It was the day before yesterday. Liz had come over to pay Emma a visit—a visit supposedly regarding the trip. Just like Elizabeth, Emma thought, remembering how she quickly went from talking about the trip to her granddaughter's college education and how Emma should help pay for it. No, make that simply pay for it, she thought. Elizabeth really had to be kidding, reminding me of the fact that I had no children of my own. How does that make me responsible for her daughter's girl? And why did it have to be Columbia? Emma complained to herself, remembering back to how Elizabeth had been the only one slated to go there those many years ago. Yep. Columbia wasn't too good for Elizabeth, while Central was more than good enough for me, Emma reminded herself.

She lay back in the comfortable chair and could feel the gentle sway of the ship. It had an almost hypnotic effect, making it easier to be lulled back into the past, almost as if the past was taking place in the here-and-now present.

Go on, Emma, she heard Elizabeth say inside her head. Put a little something up for someone else for once in your life. You're the one who got all the breaks. You're the one with the big writing career. Why can't you help Emily out? Or maybe I should make that, why won't you help Emily out? You were lucky enough to be adopted into this family. You owe it to the family to do your part, especially after you refused to help me run our father's law firm. You saw what that did. You caused it to crumble just as if you had sabotaged it yourself.

No, I didn't, Emma thought back. That was all your fault, Liz. If you hadn't been such a schemer, I would have loved to come to work there. But like everything else that took place a long time ago concerning you, you messed it up. You must be going senile. Don't you remember? You're the one who had me kept out of the firm in the first place. It's like it never ended with you. You had our father wrapped around your little finger, and you always seemed to use that against me. So don't give me that about me causing the firm to go bust, it was you. And another thing on that topic since you brought it up, it was you who talked him into going to live with his brother Jim down in Florida. That was really smart, Liz. You got rid of him so you could have absolute power at the firm, and then you proceeded to use that power to kill off the golden goose by your own sheer incompetence. Nice going, Liz. And now you're coming to me for money. Explain something to me here, won't you? Why the hell should I give you a dime? I also remember you telling Father that I had discovered my birth mother. You pulled off that little number to get me kicked out of the family. You do recall that, I know you do. But that wasn't good enough. Then you tried tracking my birth mother down for heaven only knows what reason. Thankfully you failed at that one, although I'm sure she would have seen right through you before you even got to first base.

Yeah, but you stole my boyfriend from me, the one I wanted to marry. You remember Steve Walsh? My guy who turned into your guy just to spite me. That was really nice, Emma. You showed just how shrewd and rotten you can be all at the same time. So now that we've had our one millionth fight, what do you say? I haven't got much time. I've got to get going. I feel a chill in the air and I don't want to catch anything. Not at this stage. I was sick most of last year, and you only showed up once to check on how I was doing. What a sister. Anyway, if you're going to help Emily, I would appreciate it as would her mother. If you won't help, she'll get by. Look at you. You did. You got by. Just to let you know, no one here is begging for anything, Elizabeth said, trying to stand her ground.

The ship rolled on, and the warm sun was making Emma drowsy. Too bad, she thought, she and Liz all these years, as she stretched out and turned over on her side. If only things had been different, she pined as sleep began to take its hold. If only we had been more like friends. All that time wasted..., Emma lamented, as she drifted off to sleep.

I

"Emma, come on, darling. Time to get up, sleepyhead," her mother said to her while she was opening the window blind.

Patricia Molloy was an attractive but not flashy-looking brunette, who relished her role as a mother and homemaker. Having grown up with six siblings herself, she had always desired a large family of her own. The little girl rolled over, and then Emma ducked her head under the covers.

"I know you're under there," Patricia playfully called to her. The bed didn't move. A few seconds went by, and Pat's voice become firmer. "All right, young lady, up you go. Your sister has been up for almost twenty minutes, so up you go now."

Elizabeth quietly stepped into the room. She was only a bit better-looking than ordinary and was one year older than Emma. Patricia pulled on the covers, and Emma slowly rose to her feet with a look of trepidation while her long, flowing blond hair fell over her shoulders, giving her the look of an angel.

"It'll be fine, Emma," her mother said.

"But I don't want to go to school," Emma insisted.

"Come on, now, Emma. We've been over this many times before. Besides, it'll be fun. Ask Liz. She likes school and she liked her first day. Now go wash up and come down to breakfast, and we'll have no more of this 'I hate school' stuff. Besides, how do you know? You haven't even tried it, silly," her mother implored.

"Yeah, Em, how do you know?" Elizabeth chimed in.

Patricia left the room, and Liz moved toward her little sister. "Quit feeling sorry for yourself. Nobody's going to hurt you. You may even like it," Liz told her. Then she paused and thought about it. "No, you're not going to like it. No, not you," she taunted and she walked out of the room.

Almost ten minutes went by before Pat called up the stairs to her youngest daughter. "Come on down, Emma, your breakfast is getting cold. And make sure you've brushed those teeth," she said.

Emma's father, Tom Molloy, was seated at the head of the dining room table. He was a tall, stocky, powerful-looking man in his upper forties with short brown hair showing some signs of graying. He was neatly dressed in a dark-blue business suit with a red tie and a pressed white handkerchief neatly folded and tucked into his jacket pocket. The man looked impeccable as he lorded over his kingdom and the subjects who made up his court. Tom Molloy was a very successful corporate attorney, who had opened his own private practice and done very well. Several of his clients were well-known names, while others were just plain wealthy.

"Pat, I want to know if she's ever going to get down here, or are we back to that school crap again? I thought you had that one buttoned up. Now let's eat with her or without her. I'm in a hurry this morning. I told you I have to go before Judge Nelson downtown this morning, and Flushing isn't exactly around the corner," he pontificated.

"Come on, Emma, everybody is waiting," Patricia called up the stairs. "Sometimes I think I'm being forced into getting a full-time housekeeper who can cook with the way this family operates," Tom pouted to his wife.

"Good morning, Daddy," Elizabeth said in her cutest, little voice while sitting down in the high-back mahogany chair next to her father.

Tom smiled at her. "Good morning, sweetie," he replied, picking up his paper.

Pat came in from the kitchen and dutifully served them their breakfast—a large omelet for Tom and a somewhat smaller one for Liz. "I'll go up and see what's keeping her, Tom. You wait here and eat your breakfast," she said as she left the dining room and headed up the stairs. Patricia stepped into Emma's room and saw her half-dressed and sitting—no, crying on the bed. "There now, sweetheart, you mustn't cry. Where's my big girl? Everything's going to be all right, I promise."

Emma hugged her mother and then looked up into her eyes. "All right, Mommy, I'll try. I'll try for you, but it's just that I'm afraid."

"Afraid of what?" her mother answered.

"I'm afraid I won't have any friends there and that I'll be all alone, and nobody will like me," Emma confided.

"Patricia, will you get a move on?" Tom yelled up.

Pat looked down at her daughter. "Come on, let's show Daddy, Emma. Let's show him my big girl," she gently coaxed.

Emma's face perked up. "All right, Mommy, we'll show him. We'll show Daddy," she said.

Pat kissed her on the forehead and gave her a hug. "Now you move along, and I'll see you downstairs," Pat persuaded, and she left the room and descended the staircase and walked over to her husband. "Tom, I think she'll be fine now. Don't worry. She'll be down in a minute," Pat reported.

Tom didn't look up. "Did you get my other suit back from the cleaners?" he asked his wife.

"Yes, it's back. You're all set, you'll be ready to go," Pat answered, turning her head and watching, while her youngest entered the room. Emma walked over to where her father was seated.

"How do I look, Daddy?" Emma asked him.

Tom pulled his head out of the paper and looked at his daughter. "Well, I'd say you look very spiffy for your first day of school, young lady," he answered, getting up from his chair. Patricia went to the hall closet by the front door and got him his hat and turned and handed it to him. He leaned down and kissed her on the cheek. "Well, off I go, off to slay another dragon," he proudly exclaimed. He opened the door and turned back to Pat. "That is if I can ever make it downtown before ten o'clock." Then he kissed her on the cheek again and walked out of the house.

Patricia went back to the dining room to check on things and then into the kitchen. She returned to the girls and gave Emma her bowl of cereal. "Better hurry, Emma, or you'll miss the bus," Pat said.

Emma remained quiet and just kept on eating. "Mother's right, Emma. We could miss the bus if you don't get cracking. I'm going to run upstairs for a moment and grab my light sweater, and then we've got to go, okay?" she asserted.

Emma looked wonderful in her Catholic school tartan uniform. "I'll do my very best, Mommy. I promise I will," she said, taking a few bites of cereal before getting up from the table. She walked over with her mother to her sister, who was standing at the front door.

Pat leaned down and gave them both a kiss. She told them to wait a moment and ran back to the kitchen and returned with their two lunch boxes and handed them to the girls. "Remember, Liz, I'm counting on you to take care of your sister," she said.

4

"I will, Mommy," Liz replied.

The two girls started down the street for the bus stop just as the big yellow machine roared past them. "Nice going, Emma," Liz snapped. "Now we must walk all the way to school because of you," she complained. Emma remained silent and just kept walking forward with her head down, giving the impression of something of a dirge to anyone passing by. The ten-block walk seemed to take forever to Liz.

"What teacher do you think I'll get? Will it be Sister Veronica or Mrs. Wilson?" Emma asked.

"Our last name is how they will determine it," Liz answered her. "It's about the letter M, as in Molloy. You don't know all of your letters yet, I don't think, so it's like this. The first half of the alphabet will probably go to Sister Veronica, and the other half will probably go to Mrs. Wilson," Liz told her, exuding an air of intellectual superiority.

"Then since Molloy is in the middle of the alphabet, I could go either way," Emma interjected.

Liz was surprised by her remark. "Yes, that's true. You could go either way, and lucky for you if you end up with Mrs. Wilson because the girls in the other class told me that nobody liked Sister Veronica because she was too strict, and anyone caught talking would get their hand slapped by her wooden ruler."

Emma's face deepened with concern. "You mean she just slaps the ruler across your bare hand if you're talking?" she asked in amazement.

"Worse than that," Liz replied. "She sometimes even washes your mouth out with a bar of soap. And I don't just mean the boys, she even does it to girls too."

Emma was positively shaken. "You had her last year, right? And you didn't get hit or eat soap, did you?" she sheepishly asked.

"No, stupid. I certainly did not. Not one time. Sister Veronica thought I was good because I never caused her any trouble. But you had better not get her. You even have Daddy angry at you so often that… Well, you just better be careful if you get stuck with Sister Veronica, and that's all there is to it. Okay?"

Emma didn't utter a word. They continued their walk for several more minutes and could finally see the filled schoolyard up ahead in the distance. Emma's face looked frozen with fear as they finally entered through the tall chain-link gate.

"That's her over there, Em," Liz said, pointing to an old tired-looking nun, who was somewhat hunched over. "Good luck, Em. You have to go over there, where she is. I'll meet you here later when they give us lunch period," Liz calmly said, and then she walked away. The little girl felt bewildered. She thought about her promise to her mother and summoned up all the courage that was in her as she stepped forward into the great unknown.

It was almost half past three when the front doorbell rang. Patricia put down her sewing basket and got off the couch and answered it. She opened the door and looked down, and a big smile radiated over her face.

"Well, how was it for my two little students at school today?" she proudly asked.

Liz pushed past her and entered the foyer. Emma reached up for her mother's hand and grabbed it, and they both walked into the living room followed by Liz. "Sit down and tell me all about it, girls. You go first, Emma, since it was your first day." Liz bristled.

"It went very good, Mommy," Emma innocently proclaimed while her mother pushed aside her sewing box.

"Well, who is your teacher, Emma? What's her name?" Pat asked.

"She got Mrs. Wilson," Liz answered with a smirk.

"Well, that's nice," Pat responded. "Do you like her, Emma? Is she nice?" Pat asked her.

"Oh yes, Mommy. Mrs. Wilson is wonderful. I like her very much," she told her mother. A wide, beaming smile came over Pat's face. Well, that's a relief, she thought to herself. Then she turned her attention to Elizabeth. "Aren't you happy for Emma, Liz?" Pat asked.

"Yes, Mommy, I suppose I am," she glumly replied.

Pat overlooked her attitude. "And how did my big girl make out today?" Pat asked her.

Liz took a moment before answering. "I did good, too, I guess. I got Mrs. Johnson, she's new."

"Do you like her?" Pat asked.

"I'm not sure, but I think so. I think we will be able to get along," Liz told her.

Pat was happy with the news. "Now you, girls, go upstairs and get changed and hang up those uniforms, and then you can go out and play until dinner. I have some things to do and then I'll make dinner for you two before your father gets home. He's going to be late, so he'll be eating when he gets home. Now off with you, and oh yes, homework. Did either of you get any?" Pat asked.

"No, Mommy," they each responded.

"Good, and oh, by the way, we'll be eating about five thirty, so don't be late," she said as the two girls headed for the staircase to their rooms.

Well, so far, so good, Pat thought to herself as she went back to her sewing.

II

The snow had stopped falling sometime earlier. Dusk had already taken hold, accentuating the amber color shining down on the snow from the city streetlight. The wind was down; it was a calm, peaceful setting outside of the Molloy home that early Christmas Eve—the second one after Emma started first grade. No one was out walking. The children were all home from school, and the working adults, for the most part, were already home with them, trying to feel like children themselves, at least for a little while. The phone rang, and Patricia Molloy left her family in the living room and walked into the kitchen to answer it.

"Hello, Mrs. Molloy, and Merry Christmas," the cheery woman's voice said. "This is Kathy at Carbone's Bakery. We'll be able to send over the extra pie you called about, the coconut custard. It should be sent to you within the hour. I'm sorry it can't be sooner, but we've been swamped," she said.

Patricia thanked her and got off the phone and went in to tell everybody. "Guess what we're getting," she exclaimed.

Only Emma could break her concentration from the TV set and look up. "What is it, Mommy?" she responded.

"We're getting our favorite from the bakery. The coconut custard you've all been asking for, well, guess what? It's on its way here for dinner," Pat triumphantly told them.

Emma smiled at her and then turned her attention back to the set. "Well, isn't anyone going to say anything?" Patricia pined.

"That's wonderful, dear," her husband called over from his big easy chair. Tom put his drink down on the side table and sighed. The six-o'clock news was about to begin, and he didn't want the girls hearing too much, given the cold war and all the stories on television about the possibility of a nuclear war with the Soviets. "Go in and help your mother," he ordered them.

Emma and Elizabeth both got off the couch and went over to Patricia. Then Tom motioned with his right hand for his wife to come to him. "And do me a favor… This time, make it a strong one. Its Christmas, for crying out loud," he demanded, handing her his empty glass.

Pat took the glass without saying a word and turned back to the girls, and then they went into the kitchen.

"Why does Daddy drink so much?" Liz asked her mother.

"Is it because he doesn't like us?" Emma innocently inquired.

"You two girls just stir the pots on the stove for now and be careful. They're hot," she told them while trying to figure out in her mind how to answer the drinking question in the most diplomatic way possible. Pat stepped away from them and went into the dining room. Surely, there must be a good answer, she thought. "How are my two girls coming in there?" she called out to them.

"Oh, we're doing all right, Mommy," Liz replied. "Only, Emma's getting a little sloppy. She almost spilled twice, and she just about knocked the pot over too," she informed her mother.

"Well, you two better be careful in there, that stove is hot. Now make sure you practice what I've taught you," Pat cautioned as she went back into the kitchen to make her husband that drink. Then she brought it over to him. "Here you go, Tom, but for my sake, make it your last one for tonight, won't you?" she pleaded.

Tom looked up and smiled at her. "Okay, baby, I'll take it easy," he promised. Pat pretended to be convinced. "And I'll tell you what, I'll tell you something else, my little friend. I've got something hidden away that will make this the best Christmas ever, you'll see. The best ever," he boasted, sipping his drink.

Pat relaxed a bit. She sat down on the chair next to his and grabbed his hand in nervous anticipation. "You're not going to get it out of me quite that fast, my dear. It's a surprise, and I want it to stay that way until just the right moment," he playfully teased her. Pat was overcome with curiosity. She thought that they had covered all the bases as far as the girls went. Then Tom pulled her by the arm onto his lap. "Just like old times." he mused with an all too ingenious look in his eye.

Pat twisted in his lap and playfully grabbed onto his neck with her two hands. "You better tell me, or else, Mr. Molloy...," she theatrically threatened with a large grin appearing on her face.

Tom sensed that he had her. "Okay, I'll tell you what, Mrs. Molloy. I'll tell you confidentially, but in return, I get just one more scotch, and that will be it for the evening. Agreed?" he asked.

Pat thought for a second and decided, What the heck, he's looking like he's in pretty good shape, and it is Christmas after all. "You're on, partner," she said, surprising him to his core while at the same time making him feel victorious.

"I got a bike," he blurted.

"A bike?" Pat questioned in a surprised tone.

"Yes, a bike, and it's a real beauty," Tom bragged. "It's a girl's bike, but it's not really a bike—no, it's an English racer, you know, one of those bikes with the three-speed gear shift and the two hand brakes," he expounded.

Pat looked puzzled. "The last time I checked, the term 'a bike' was the singular form, you know, a bike, as in one bike. One bike, two daughters, well, you're a lawyer, you get the picture. So tell me you meant to say two bikes, not a bike, please," she insisted.

Tom took a sip from his drink. "Get off me, Pat, you're getting heavy," he complained.

Pat stood up and hovered over him. "You didn't. You didn't bring home two bikes, did you?" she interrogated. She took a step closer but then turned and walked over to the TV and turned off the set. But there was no answer coming from him, so she tried again. "Tom, I know the bike is for Elizabeth, but how could you not get one for Emma also? She's your daughter too. Tell me you at least got something extra for her, Tom. Tell me, Tom," she demanded.

"I got something for her," he sheepishly responded. "But I didn't get her a bike, if that's what you mean. I got her a scarf. She's really going to—"

"She's really going to like it, is that what you're going to tell me? Well, that's pathetic, Tom. You're acting as if you don't even care about her, let alone love her. You seem to not care about her at all, and this really proves it. Why are you being like this, Tom?" she challenged.

Tom finished his drink and slammed the glass down on the end table. "All right, Ms. Righteous, I'm sick of this. I'll tell you what's eating me, I'll let you know, and maybe it's something you already should know without me having to tell you. It's Tom, our son. It's about Tom," he screamed at her, almost crying but still loud enough to be heard throughout the entire house. "It's Tom, you idiot," he reiterated. "Don't you know by now, haven't you seen it? I mean, every time I look at Emma, I think of him. And contrary to popular belief around here, she just isn't making the grade as a good, surrogate replacement for that boy, my boy, my son, my real son. And it only gets worse at Christmas," he declared, looking straight at his wife with daggers coming out of both eyes.

Pat was flushed with emotions. She took a deep breath and stepped closer to her husband and began to cry. "I'm sorry I've made your life so miserable by wanting that little girl, Tom," she humbly told him, but he didn't appear to be moved. "Tom, you know, you remember how much we both wanted to have children."

"Children of our own," he interrupted.

Pat caught herself and took another deep breath. "Yes, that's true, Tom, but we both agreed to adopt after the stillbirth."

"Call him by his name, Pat. His name was Tom, okay, and thank you. Call him by his name and don't you ever refer to our son as a stillbirth again. Do you understand?" he exploded.

Pat was taken aback. She took a moment before answering; she could see that he truly was in pain with a pain that she had never seen before—no, it was more like an anguish, an anguish that reached down into his inner core. A large plate crashed in the kitchen, but Pat couldn't move; she remained frozen, fixated, staring at a man whose grief knew no bounds.

"Why then, Tom? Why then did you agree to do it? To adopt, I mean," she carefully asked.

Tom took a moment before answering, telling himself that it really didn't matter anymore what he told her, so he decided to tell her the truth. "I did it to shut you up, Pat. There, are you happy? I did it to shut you and all your endless crying back then the hell up. Don't you understand? You were literally driving me crazy, so I thought this might be an acceptable solution. Boy, was I ever wrong because every time I see her, I see him, and I don't like it, Pat, because for me, it's like I can never let go even a little, and I have never really had any damn peace," he divulged to his wife as he got up and walked out of the room.

Elizabeth and Emma were a few feet apart from each other in the kitchen. Emma was visibly shaken as she stooped down to pick up the broken shards from the plate hitting the floor. She looked up at Elizabeth with a puzzled look on her face. "What does adopt mean?" she asked her.

Elizabeth didn't know and wasn't interested. "You better get that cleaned up before Daddy sees it, Emma. Daddy's really going to get sore if he sees that," she insisted.

Emma nodded her head, thinking her sister was right and that this had to be over with quickly, but she couldn't get the adopt question out of her young mind. Patricia walked into the kitchen and looked right at her.

"What happened in here?" she whimsically asked, trying to change the subject.

"I'll tell you, Mommy," Elizabeth volunteered. "We were being careful, but then we heard Daddy, and, well, Emma just smashed the plate down."

At first, Pat became angry, but then it quickly dawned on her that perhaps Emma might have heard too much, since she and Tom had never told their children about adoption. "Well, Emma, is that true?" Pat questioned her.

Emma looked clearly intimidated. "No, Mommy, no, the plate slipped, honest, it slipped," she told her mother.

Elizabeth wasn't having any of it. "She dropped it deliberately when she heard I was getting a bicycle and she wasn't. Daddy made that pretty clear," she added.

Pat felt like she was painted into a corner. "Emma, if that's true, then I'm afraid you'll have to go to your room. So answer me, is that true," Pat demanded.

Emma was speechless. She was overcome with fear inside, sensing that something was deeply wrong, which she just couldn't explain, and that she was somehow the reason, that it was all her own fault. Feeling somewhat dazed by everything, the youngster just couldn't think of anything to say to defend herself.

"Then go to your room and go to your room now until I call you, Emma," Pat sternly ordered her before explaining away Tom's behavior to her older daughter.

III

It was a nice, clear, spring morning in Flushing after a heavy overnight rain. The air was fresh, the bright, early morning sun was out, and the few remaining snow mounds from another long winter were almost all gone. Emma and Elizabeth were walking together to St. Rita's grammar school. They were several years older now and were both beginning to feel some of the strain associated with a difficult time in one's life. Things were certainly changing, perhaps a bit faster for Elizabeth, but life was becoming different for them both.

"Take it easy, Em. We're not going to be late, we've got enough time," Elizabeth pronounced to her worried sister just as a large snowball crashed to the ground a few feet in front of them. Even though startled, Elizabeth quickly looked over her left shoulder and saw one of the boys from her sixth-grade class on the other side of the street with a big grin on his face.

"Hey, Liz, how about meeting me after school today over at the candy store?" he called out to her.

But Elizabeth wasn't interested and just kept walking. "Don't look at him, Em. He's a jerk. I wouldn't be caught dead talking to him at the water fountain, never mind go out on a date with him," she curtly said.

"Elizabeth, how did you get to get so many boys to like you?" Emma asked.

"Personality, looks, brains, charm," I guess. "Did I leave anything out?" Liz said, chuckling to herself.

Emma felt somewhat proud to be the sister of and the one walking next to one of the most popular kids in the whole school. As they neared the schoolyard, they could see that the other kids were all still outside. "See, Em, I told you we had plenty of time to get here," Elizabeth gloated as three of her girlfriends approached them. "So there he was again this morning," Liz boasted to her waiting audience, who seemed to dangle on her every word.

"And what happened this time?" Angela asked her.

"Did he try to kiss you?" Kathy added.

Elizabeth laughed. "No, the stupid jerk threw a snowball in front of me and then asked me to meet him over at the candy store after school today."

"Are you going to meet him?" Emma foolishly asked her sister, causing a stir among the other girls.

"Come on, Liz. Leave your little sister here and let's hear the rest of it where we don't have to listen to something so dumb," Angela told her.

Elizabeth nodded and then looked at Emma. "Okay. So I'll see you later, Em. I'll see you at home after school," she told her as she began to lead her three friends to the other side of the yard to cover the latest. Then Liz abruptly stopped and turned back toward her sister. "And to answer your question, Emma, no, I'm not going to meet him, so don't say anything to Mom," she ordered and then left her standing there, feeling as though she was the odd man out.

"Hi, Em, what have you been doing?" a friendly-sounding voice called out. It was Janice Donaldson, maybe the least popular girl in fifth grade. With braided pigtails and thick-rimmed brown glasses, she certainly wasn't using her looks to her advantage.

"Oh, hi, Janice," Emma answered, moving toward her. "I've been doing nothing, really. Just my homework and working on my composition, I guess," Emma told her.

"Yeah, me too. Pretty much the same as you. The composition isn't any fun. Who wants to write about Mrs. Robbins' old, dead, history figures, anyway?" she lamented.

Emma took exception. "Oh, I kind of don't mind that so much. I like writing but yeah, I guess you're right. Mrs. Robbins could have let us select other more interesting topics," Emma agreed.

"Say, what's with Elizabeth, Em? Boy, did she give you the brush off. That wasn't so nice," Janice sympathetically asked her friend.

Emma was embarrassed. "Oh, that, well, that was about Donald, Donald Parsons. He keeps asking her to meet or go on a date or something. She's not mad at me. She just doesn't want to be reminded about him, and so you see, I was with her when he showed up and...you know what I mean," Emma tried explaining.

Janice really wasn't following her. "Come on, Emma, let's go inside, and I'll show you what I wrote so far before the other kids go in. Maybe we can help each other and both get a better grade," Janice suggested.

"What gives with her?" Kathy asked Elizabeth as they found a place to perch on the far side of the schoolyard.

"I mean, doesn't she get it?" the third girl stated. Liz was not in the mood to defend her sister and didn't want her sister's low stature to reflect on her with her friends.

"Look, you guys," Liz responded, "We just so happen to live in the same house, that's all, nothing I can do about it. I have to walk with her in the morning, my mother insists even though I keep telling her that it's ridiculous, but it's, like, my mom's on another planet and I'm not going to be allowed to get rid of her for some time now or maybe forever from the looks of things," Liz bemoaned.

"Well, I hope for your sake it's not forever," Kathy taunted, causing the other two girls to instantly laugh as the bell rang for the students to enter the building.

When Liz got home from school later that afternoon, Patricia was on the phone with a friend. "All right, Mary, we'll be over Saturday, about seven. Tom and I have both been looking forward to it. Give Jim our best and please tell him we're pulling for him with that promotion. Goodbye and see you then," she sweetly said as Liz impatiently stormed over to her.

"How was school today?" Pat asked her, putting the phone down. She could see that Liz was pretty well worked up, upset about something, but she had seen worse, Pat told herself.

"I just can't take it anymore."

"Oh, come on now, Liz. Sister Cecilia isn't so bad. You told me so yourself," Pat interrupted, hoping that this wasn't going to be about Emma once more.

"Mother, let's get real for once. I walked into the school-yard this morning and got ambushed by Angela and Kathy, and of course, Emma is there with me, and she, of course, can't keep her big mouth shut. She immediately tells them that Donald Parsons tried getting me to go with him to the store after school, and they—"

"What's so terrible about that, Liz? Emma must have really admired you for getting asked out, that's all," Pat said, cutting her off.

Liz began breathing harder. "Mother, you simply don't understand. He's a Neanderthal. It was so embarrassing.

18

And Angela even goes around saying that he isn't even smart enough to make it to Neanderthal. So don't you see? That dimwit sister of mine has ruined me in front of Angela and Kathy," she exaggerated.

Pat could see her point on a certain level but was more interested in having her look after Emma as much as possible, especially while they were at school. "I'm sure the girls realize that you and Donald, I mean, that you don't like him and that's that," Pat suggested.

Liz wasn't buying any of it. "It's a lot different today, Mother, than when you were a girl. It's a whole different, modern world now, and I just don't think you get it. Emma is old enough to at least go to school on her own. So there you have it. I'm through being the adoption agency for you and for Emma. From now on, she's on her own," Liz asserted.

Pat was becoming angry, but she thought to herself it might just be better to take the matter up with Tom rather than punch back at that moment. Besides, she thought, she wasn't really sure how he would come down on it. So for now, it had better wait, Pat reasoned. "Liz, I'm going to take this up with your father just as soon as possible," she told her, trying to look as confident as she possibly could.

"Daddy, he'll agree with me, you'll see," Liz smugly rebutted before walking off in a huff. Pat feared her daughter was probably right as she watched her storm off.

That evening, Tom Molloy sat down at the table for dinner before Emma came down from her room. "So, Liz, your mother told me that you're all grown up now and that you can't be bothered with taking your sister to school anymore," he dismissively said, putting his glass of scotch down and thinking more about what there was to eat than the pending problem his family was facing. But Liz was very good at playing her father, and as usual, she was ready for him.

"You look nice tonight, Daddy, but you don't want me to tell you that right now when my whole life is about ready to get kicked under the bus," she whimpered with a slightly sad expression on her face.

Tom looked over at her, thinking it might be a little more serious than Patricia had led him to believe. "I don't see how your sister tagging along can be such a burden. She's rather quiet, almost an introvert, I would say. I could see if she was really loud, precocious, or even very talented, but she's not, she's none of these," he gently said, trying to humor her.

Liz just pouted. "Daddy, that's just it. She's not very bright and she always ends up saying the wrong things at the wrong time. It never fails, and it's always at my expense. I just don't need it anymore," she complained to her father, who looked as though he might be coming around.

Pat entered the room, holding a large meat plate. "Liz, don't you think this whole thing is a bit much?" Pat chided, receiving a glaring stare in return from her daughter.

"You just don't understand, Mother, you never do. I'm not going to be made the laughingstock with my friends because of Emma, or anyone else, for that matter," she exclaimed.

"Well, if your friends act the way you say they act, then why do you keep them as friends? Why don't you get new ones, real ones, instead?" Pat reasoned, hitting a nerve with her daughter, who began to turn somewhat red.

"Pat, maybe Liz has a point," Tom suggested, coming to Liz's defense. "And besides, Pat, think of it, Liz is a year older, and she is entering a critical stage of her life, and she doesn't need a lot of distractions if she's going to keep her grades up and get into law school someday. So maybe give it a rest and tell me something important. Tell me what you've got on that plate and let's get started with dinner," he told her, trying to change the subject as quickly as possible.

Pat put the plate down and returned to the kitchen. "Thank you, Daddy," Liz politely said to him. "You're right about my studies, it is difficult enough without Emma's extracurricular baloney. I need to keep her from getting to me. I do so much want to make you happy, Daddy. I do so much want to go to law school and make you proud of me, Daddy," she coddled as Emma walked over to the table and sat down.

"Emma, pass me the meat, please," Tom asked her. She obediently did as asked as Pat came back in with a bowl and sat down. "What's new at school, Emma?" her father asked her.

"Oh, not too much. I'm writing a history composition on Abraham Lincoln, and it's coming along all right, I guess," she answered.

"Mother, aren't you going to say anything?" Liz demanded. Patricia remained calm. "Eat your dinner before it gets cold," she tersely replied, carefully looking across the table at her husband for his reaction. But Tom was too busy playing with his mashed potatoes to want to say anything, so Pat felt safe. The room became silent for a moment, and then Emma lifted her head up and looked across the table at Liz.

"It's okay, Liz, if you want to go to school by yourself. I heard what you said to Daddy just now when I was coming down the stairs. It's okay. Besides, I have to make room for my own friends, my own schoolwork, and lots of other stuff too," she defensively told Liz. Emma glanced over at her father and saw Tom look away from her and over toward Liz. Emma then turned her head toward Pat, looking for her approval. Pat thought to herself that perhaps she should just let nature take its course rather than have another big family argument, but she also instinctively didn't want to see Emma get left behind and treated as though she were second class.

"Emma, darling, if you feel that way, then you shouldn't have to bother with it anymore," Pat told her, trying to bolster her self-esteem as diplomatically as possible. "Why, I was pretty much on my own from my older sister when I was your age, and it all worked out for the better, and your aunt Doris and I are the best of friends to this day," Pat encouraged her.

"It's okay, Mom, it's fine," Emma quietly told her mother as she hurtfully looked across the table at Liz, hoping for some kind of an apology or change of heart. But nothing like that came from her sister, who just looked away from her and over toward her father.

It seemed to Emma that the meal took forever. Finally, it ended. "That was a terrific dinner tonight, Pat," Tom said, walking into the kitchen. "Nobody can make pot roast the way you do," he praised her, pouring himself a short drink on the kitchen counter.

"I hope that'll be all for tonight," Pat insisted, stepping closer toward him.

"That's all for tonight. Besides, I'm fine. You knew I could hold my liquor when you married me, and so far, nothing's changed in that department, I'm happy to say."

"Tom, you've got to pay more attention to Emma. Oh, I know you picture Liz becoming a great lawyer someday and I certainly believe she's quite capable, but think for a moment about Emma. She idolizes you, Tom, and she has brains and ability, too, not that it should even matter," Pat argued. "Why don't you encourage her toward law also? She's a good student, look at her report card sometime and you'll see. Besides, she seems to enjoy writing those compositions whenever they come up, and I know myself from my own school days that writing those darn compositions was nothing but a real chore. Lawyers write a lot, I know that from watching you over the years, so how about it? Encourage her, Tom. She needs direction, everyone does," Pat pleaded.

Tom took a sip from his drink. "You're right, Pat, I'll tell her to set some goals, to try law if she likes. I'll even tell her that she could make herself into a great lawyer someday with hard work and dedication. You're right, I'll do it. Now let me finish this, and oh yes, it's getting late. Can we get up to bed now?" he asked her as he gulped his drink and started out of the room, thinking to himself that Liz was really right, that she should be able to break free of Emma if she really wanted to.

IV

It was a warm, sunny, early September afternoon. The day's classes had all wrapped up, and several of the students were preparing for their various after-school activates at Francis Lehman. The track behind the high school was brimming with runners stretching and sprinting, while inside the oval the high jumpers worked on their technique. The woman's track coach was a pleasant-looking woman in her late thirties, dressed in her sweatpants and top and looking like she had seen it all in high school track. Emma walked out one of the rear school building doors with her friend and headed over to the coach.

"Ms. Hartman, this is the girl I told you about. I'd like you to meet Emma, Emma Molloy," Betty told her. "We've done some running on the weekends together, and I have to tell you, Coach, that she's really fast. Emma's the real deal in the sprints," she told her. Emma shrugged it off.

"So, Emma, it's always nice to meet someone who wants to become a part of our team. Have you run anywhere that I might know about?" Coach Hartman asked. Emma just shook her head.

"Get her on the track, Coach, and take a look. You'll see what I mean," Betty confidently proclaimed.

"Okay, young lady…ah, you're a freshman here, like Betty, I take it."

"That's right," Betty enthusiastically jumped in.

"Okay then, let's see what you've got," the coach said, pointing with her finger toward a starting block as she reached into her pocket and pulled out a stopwatch. Emma nervously walked over to the block. She reached up to the sky to try to loosen up and then she bent down at the waist and came up again and then pressed her right foot back against the block.

"Are you ready, Emma," Ms. Hartman shouted over, anxiously awaiting to see the results. Emma nodded. "Okay then, give me forty on three. It's the first yellow marker ahead of you," the coach ordered. Emma took a deep breath. "One, two, three," the coach counted out loud, and then Emma was off like a shot, tearing up the track in her short sprint to the finish.

"Like a blur," Betty told the coach.

Ms. Hartman stood there almost in disbelief. "She's under four seven, maybe four six, I don't exactly know, but she's fast. She's extremely fast," Hartman concluded.

Betty seemed quite pleased with herself. "See? I told you so," she proudly exclaimed to the coach.

"What did you say her last name was, Betty?" Sylvia asked.

"Molloy with two L's. She has a sister here, Elizabeth. She goes by Liz. She's a sophomore."

Sylvia tried to reach back in her mind, and then she came up with it. "Oh yeah, that's right," the coach mused out loud. "Liz Molloy. She came out last year, ran the fifteen hundred, I think. She wasn't very good, lasted only about a week or so, if my memory serves me. No, she certainly wasn't anything like her sister here," she said as Emma returned to where they were both standing.

"How'd I do?" Emma humbly asked the coach, hoping to hear that she hadn't disqualified herself already.

Sylvia's face beamed with a big smile. "I hope you're planning on joining us, Emma. You've got it, you're a natural," she told her.

"Yeah, Emma, you were great, you were terrific," Betty enthusiastically added.

A small smile crept over Emma's face. "Then I was okay, I was good?" she blurted out, trying to suppress her doubts and really believe in what they were telling her.

Sylvia put her arms around her, and gave her a self-assuring hug and then looked her in the eye. "You were really good, Emma. Come, let's stop this foolishness and get to work. Emma, you've made the team. Now you two girls take a couple of laps, and after that, I'll give you a couple of exercises that you can do, and oh yes, Emma, you'll need to stop by my office after practice or in the morning and sign the roster. Now get going, you two," the coach told them.

The girls walked away, and Emma felt something well up inside; she was beaming with a radiant feeling she had never known before. They came up to just before the first turn on the asphalt track, and Betty broke the silence.

"Well, aren't you going to say anything?" Betty asked her.

"You mean about making the team?" Emma replied.

"Yes, silly, you told me you wanted to," Betty probed.

Emma was flattered by all the attention. "I thought I might make it, but I wasn't sure."

"Well, aren't you happy?" her friend asked her.

"Of course, I'm happy. Who wouldn't be happy?" she said as they walked past the first turn. "I'm happy, but I just don't know, with school and all. I just don't know if I can make the commitment, that's all," Emma told her.

"You've really got to be kidding, Emma. You've got talent, real talent. Don't throw it away. I'm careful about my studies also, but I'm going to stick with the team. My father says it's real important to have some credible extracurricular activities in order to get into a good college, not just any college. And he's a lawyer, he knows about all that stuff."

Emma's ears perked up. "Your dad's a lawyer?" she questioned, picturing her own father in her head.

"Yeah, and a good one," Betty replied. "Anyway, Emma, you really ought to think about it. You don't want to end up in Central College with the rest of the rejects," Betty flatly stated, looking over at her. Emma looked taken aback by the comment. "I didn't mean you're like them, that you're one of the rejects," Betty apologetically told her. "But if you end up over there in that college, there's a better than fifty-fifty chance you'll become one, a reject, like all the other losers that go to that school," she quickly stated, trying to invoke a laugh from her friend.

Emma began to smile. She wanted to feel the exhilaration she had felt with Coach Hartman, but that feeling was already past waning. Yet she felt comfortable with Betty now that she saw that Betty wasn't trying to ridicule her. "All right, Betty, I'm sold. You've convinced me. Track it is," Emma firmly stated. "I'll be as reliable, I'll be dependable, I'll run the fifty, I'll run the one hundred, I'll run whatever they want me to run, but I won't go to Central College. No, that I won't do," she declared out loud with a newfound authority as she peered out into the future—her future—more hopeful than ever before.

That evening, the dinner table was set a bit earlier than usual. Tom had phoned from the office and said he wanted to bring one of his lesser-known clients home for a casual meet and greet. Emma was up in her room lying face up on the bed. She was daydreaming about the events that had taken place that afternoon on the track. She kept trying to picture herself running the sprint over and over, going faster and faster, but the picture broke up again and again, and she could only really think about what Betty had told her about her father.

It must be nice to have a dad like Betty's, Emma thought. She rolled over on her side among her several books strewn over the bedspread. One of the books fell to the floor, but Emma remained still on the spread, only remembering Betty's remarks. "Credible extracurricular activities," she heard Betty say her father had told her. When was the last time anyone said something like that to me, she pined as the door burst open, and Liz entered her room.

"Why don't you try knocking first?" Emma challenged.

"Oh, shut up, Emma, and listen to me," Liz said, quickly getting her sister's attention.

Emma looked intrigued. When was the last time she came in here? Emma thought to herself. She rolled herself over and sat up on the bed and faced Liz, who had an unusual look on her face, almost like a look of admiration.

"But no, that couldn't be," Emma quickly surmised.

"I heard about you out there on the track this afternoon," Liz said. Emma kept quiet, waiting to see if there was a next bombshell about ready to drop. "Yeah, Emma, I heard you were pretty good," Liz continued. Emma began to relax a little.

"I ran for Ms. Hartman, if that's what you mean," Emma admitted, trying to avoid a competition with her.

Liz pushed away one of the books and sat down on the edge of the bed. "So what are you going to do? Are you in or out? Are you going to join or not?" She grilled her. Emma took her time answering. "I'm not one hundred percent sure, but I'm not ruling it out either. Betty Williams is on it. She introduced me to Ms. Hartman."

"You like Betty, you're friends with her," Liz butted in.

Emma was surprised by the question. "Yeah, I like her. I like her a lot," Emma conceded, telling herself to stay off Betty's discussion about her father. Liz felt like she was gaining the upper hand.

"Jane Seymore says that Betty's older brother is a dope dealer. You know who Jane Seymore is, I hope," Liz instructed. Emma had heard of her, and she knew her to be the captain of the girls track team.

"What does that have to do with Betty?" Emma asked her sister, looking somewhat perplexed.

Liz got up from the bed and headed over to the door and turned back toward her sister. "You'll figure that one out for yourself, I'm sure," she told her and then she turned and headed out the door.

Emma lay back on the bed, staring faceup again. She closed her eyes and pictured Betty and heard her say again what her father had told her. No, Liz, she thought to herself. I'm not going to Central College, not for you; not for anybody else, she told herself, seeing through her sister's ruse.

A few minutes went by, and Liz returned to Emma's room; her demeanor had noticeably changed, Emma thought to herself, spotting her from the bed.

"I'm going to ask you for a favor, but if you don't want to do it, it's okay," Liz nervously said to her while still trying to maintain rank. Emma didn't answer. What could she possibly want? Emma thought to herself. Liz took a couple of steps closer. "Emma, it's okay if you don't want to do it. I can get it somewhere else if you say no."

"Just tell me what it is," Emma interrupted.

"Well, it's...it's just that I've been having a little trouble with math, and I was wondering if—"

"If I could what?" Emma jumped in.

"If you could help me. I know you're good at it, Em, and I was wondering if you would, you know, sort of help me," Liz awkwardly said.

Emma looked straight at her; she couldn't believe what she was hearing. Liz was supposed to be this all-knowing genius, and yet here she was, sniveling away because she couldn't do it. But the exhilaration quickly turned to compassion; deep down Emma didn't relish the position that her sister was in.

"Okay, Liz, you've got me on that one. But keep in mind I'm a year behind you. What if I can't do the work yet? That could happen, you know," Emma told her.

Liz just shook her head. "No, Emma, I'll have to give it to you. You're really just way too smart for that," Liz had to admit.

It was a little after six that evening when Tom arrived at the front door with his dinner guest, George Sanders, who was conservatively dressed in a dark blue suit and who was about Tom's age; he headed up a small bank in the Albany area.

"Nice-looking home, Tom. And thanks for the invite. It's nice not to have to eat out alone in the city every time I come down here," he appreciatively said.

"We'll get those contracts out by tomorrow. Just swing by the office after lunchtime, and they will be ready," Tom assured him as he opened the front door to his home. "I'm home, dear," he called out to Pat, who was already standing there to greet them. "This is George Sanders, dear, the world's greatest banker, whom I told you about, and, George, I'd like you to meet my lovely wife of thirty-something years."

"Thirty-five," Pat interjected.

"Oh yes, thirty-five," Tom corrected himself. "You see, George, I was never really quite that good with numbers. That's why I went into the law and left the numbers to the guys like you, the guys who are really good," Tom playfully ad-libbed. George had a good-natured laugh, and they all went into the living room.

"Welcome to our home, George. I'm glad you could come for dinner," Pat dutifully said to him.

"And how about that drink I promised you?" Tom asked his client.

"Make mine a scotch and water," George said.

"That'll be easy, one with and one without, Pat, if you please," Tom told her.

Pat went into the kitchen to make the drinks as the two men sat down. "Looks like the Yankees almost have it sewn up," George said. "That's the one thing I'd really like about living down here. You've got the best team in baseball practically in your own backyard. Up around Albany, we've got a pretty decent minor league team, but it's just not the same," George bantered.

Pat came back into the room and handed George his drink. "With water for you, George," she said with a smile. "Without water for you, dear," she said with a frown after turning away from her guest.

"Well, cheers and let's go Yankees," Tom toasted, holding his glass up in the air. The men each took a drink.

"Figure about ten to fifteen for dinner," Pat told them.

"You have a lovely home, Pat," George politely said. Pat smiled and thanked him and left the room.

"You'll be meeting my two daughters at dinner. They're both in high school, sophomore and freshman year," Tom said.

"Looking forward to it," George replied.

"Liz, the oldest one, well, she's already targeting law school—with my undying persuasion, of course. And Emma, well, let's just say that she hasn't made up her mind yet on anything, but from what they tell me around here, it is purported that she writes one mean composition. I don't really know if that's true, mind you, but that is the rumor," Tom related to him, sipping his drink and keeping up his end of the small talk.

George seemed amused. "You know, Tom, my wife and I have two kids, two girls also, about the same age. They keep themselves pretty well occupied also. Well, if I didn't know any better, I wouldn't take them as sisters at all. Nope, you would look at those two and think that they were simply best friends. And another nice thing that I have going is that they are both interested in medicine. So there you have it, they get along, and there's a bit of a built-in cost savings with the hand-me-downs to boot," George quipped.

"Nice going," Tom replied, raising his glass in the air and saluting him the way men do when they drink together. He took a drink and confidently nodded over to his guest. "I know what you mean with sisters," Tom confided. "They're the best. Boys are, well, you know, boys are rough to deal with sometimes. They're too headstrong at times, and they like to fight too much. I'm just happy that I have two wonderful daughters who love me and love each other. It's really nice," Tom described in one of his all-time best-selling performances.

"I couldn't agree with you more, Tom, no, I couldn't agree with you more," George concurred.

The following morning, Emma walked into Coach Hartman's office before classes started. Sylvia was very happy to see her alive with anticipation.

"I'm going to run, I mean, I'm going to join the team," Emma exclaimed. The coach's face lit up. "But I'm only going to do it provided I can keep my grades up," Emma said, thinking about the prospects of Central College in her mind.

Hartman's face dropped. She had seen too many good athletes fail for reasons other than physical ability. "Well, I'm glad you're here with us, Emma, and you do what you need to do regarding that grades matter," she said somewhat coolly.

Emma instantly picked up on the change in reception. "You don't understand, Ms. Hartman."

"From now on, it's Coach, not Ms. Hartman," Sylvia interrupted.

"Yes, Coach Hartman," Emma corrected herself. "You see, Coach, it's not that I can't do the work ordinarily. It's just that, well, sometimes I just feel out of sorts. I guess you could say I get somewhat depressed, and then studying becomes difficult, very difficult, and I just can't concentrate on things the way I should. I can't really put my finger on it, but sometimes I just feel deep down that I can't do anything well. And when it happens, I just don't have any real confidence at all," Emma disclosed.

Sylvia's heart began to warm toward her. "Emma, you're entering into what for many of us is a tough period in life. High school isn't easy, but you'll get through it, you'll be fine. Just persevere, that's all. Just don't give up," she encouraged.

"Well, I'll do my best," Emma answered.

"There, that's the spirit. Now get going to class. I don't want to get in trouble with the principal for keeping you from class even if you did run the fastest forty around here since they built the place," Sylvia jokingly said, making Emma smile.

"Thank you, Coach Hartman. And I will try my best," Emma said, turning away and leaving the office.

That same morning, the first period bell hadn't rung yet as Liz walked down the corridor with one of her closer friends in math class. Liz seemed content; things seemed to be more in order now that Emma had told her she had her back.

"It's going to be tough this semester. My sister says it gets pretty tough this year, and she's a college math major," Barbara told Liz.

"You're lucky, you Bradfords are lucky. It seems like it's not a problem. You, your sister, and your brother are all good at this stuff. It must run in your family or something, but it certainly doesn't run in mine," Liz opined.

Barbara laughed a little. "Well, I guess that's true, but—and I mean this, Liz—but if you apply yourself, you'll do fine. You're too smart for failure, and besides, you've got motivation," she added.

Liz looked a little puzzled by her friend's seemingly casual remark. "Motivation...what are you talking about, Barbara?" Liz asked.

"You know, all that stuff you told me about your father and his wanting to send you to Columbia for law school and like that. If I had a father willing to give me that, I'd surely get off my ass and crack the books. I'll be lucky if they let me go to a private college. All I ever hear is how expensive things are nowadays from my father. That's all the man knows," she continued.

Liz thought to herself this might not be so bad, that she might have a backup here who would be better than dealing with her sister, Emma. They walked farther along, and Barbara picked up the conversation.

"Say, Liz, why don't we get together after classes, say, once or twice a week, and I'll tutor you and you pay me, say, ten dollars an hour?" Barbara suggested, thinking of her own slightly impoverished situation.

"This was like manna from heaven," Liz said to herself, jealously thinking how nice life would be if she didn't have to endure even a minute of Emma telling her anything.

The first period bell rang as the girls came up to their classroom door. "When can we start," Liz quietly asked her.

"We can start today," her friend quickly answered.

"You're on then, Barbara," Liz replied, walking inside the room, feeling as though she had just closed the biggest deal of the century.

V

It was already well into the beginning of Emma's senior year at Francis Lehman High School. Emma hadn't run track for almost two years, and her grades had slipped some. The social scene hadn't gone all too well either. Betty Williams no longer talked to her, ever since she had told Coach Hartman that she just couldn't keep it up between the team and her schoolwork. And then there was the problem with her current list of friends, girls who were much too wild for her, she thought, but at least they were better than having no friends at all.

Oh, Emma could still do well at math, or any other subject for that matter, but she was finding it more and more difficult to remain focused, to be able to concentrate for more than short periods of time. And as time marched on, she knew that she was becoming even more disconnected to a clear vision, a sense of what direction her life should take. The age-old question of "what are you going to do when you grow up?" was haunting her—no, it was frightening her because she really didn't have much of a self-confident, healthy self-identity. With no real support system at home other than a roof over her head and a peer group she may have just as well have gotten rid of, Emma was hoping to somehow latch on to a purpose in life; but she couldn't, and she knew it, and it scared her. It had even gotten worse, she told herself, now that Liz was off to Columbia and living in

New York City. At least with Liz, there was always someone there to fight with, if not talk to, someone whose mere presence spurred Emma on to at least compete with and that, at least, helped her to move the ball forward and progress at something rather than lethargically attempt little or nothing. And so it was one evening when her father, Tom, sat down to dinner.

"Where's Em, Pat?" he called out to his wife, who was still in the kitchen.

"Em will be down shortly. You're a bit early. Would you like another drink, Tom?" Pat asked in a voice of quiet resignation.

"No thank you, Pat," he replied, raising her hopes that just maybe the drinking was going to slow down.

"All right then, dear. Dinner will be in just a few minutes," she called back to him in her most pleasant tone possible.

"But I'll take a rain check, Pat," he yelled back to her as her heart began to sink.

"Tom, I'm not going to go through the same old argument with you," she said, walking into the dining room, staring straight at him. "And please remember you promised after that fall you had at the McCurdy's party last week that you'd lay low. So please do that, lay low," she scolded and then returned to the kitchen.

Tom let it roll off his back. What the hell was wrong with her? She was becoming a real pain, he thought to himself just as Emma came into the room and sat down at the table.

"What's with you?" Emma asked her father, who still looked flushed from his earlier encounter.

"Mind your own business and go in and help your mother," he ordered.

Emma took off for her mother. "Hi, Mom. What's up with Dad, or should I say, Mr. Grumpy?" she asked her.

Pat began to cry. She motioned for Emma to come a bit closer. "Your father's drinking, and it's getting worse. He won't listen to me anymore. I just don't know what to do, Em, to tell you the truth," Pat divulged.

Emma didn't look surprised. "I told you he wasn't going to change even with what happened at McCurdy's, Mother," Emma said.

"What am I going to do, Emma?" Pat asked, nearing the point of despair.

Emma just looked at her, feeling nothing but sympathy and fear. "You're going to hold your ground, that's what," she told her. Pat remained silent. "You're going to make like everything is normal, but when he goes on and on about another drink, you're going to embarrass him into cleaning up his act," Emma advised.

"And how do I do that?" Pat asked.

"Very simple, Mom. Remind him of his own past, when he was building the company up from nothing and how busy he was then and how much he liked being busy. Why, now he doesn't even have to show up, and the checks in the mail! Sure, the money's real nice, but he's bored, Mom, can't you see that? And this is how he deals with it. He drinks," Emma explained.

Pat hadn't thought of it that way, but it made sense to her. "You're right, Em dear. I'll take your advice."

"Do it casually, Mom. I mean, out of the blue, start talking to him about getting more involved at the office, about building up something else even, perhaps. He's naturally good at it if you can get him motivated," Emma counseled.

"Emma, keep this between just you and me. Liz doesn't need to know anything about this. I don't want to upset her. She's got enough to worry about starting at Columbia this year," Pat said.

Emma felt a twinge. "You don't have to worry about that, Mom. We hardly talk anymore. She's really too busy for me these days ever since you and Dad hired that tutor for her to push up her grades. And oh yeah, get her prepped for those SATs. No, Mom, you needn't worry there, you needn't worry about Liz. I certainly won't say anything, that's for sure," Emma told her as she turned and left.

"Emma, go ask your mother to come in here, please," Tom said to her as she was passing by.

"Ask her yourself," Emma snapped back while proceeding to the staircase, heading up to her room for a good cry on the bed.

Tom got up and went into the kitchen. "What's up with her?" Tom demanded.

Pat just shook her head. "Tom, let me say something to you that just now dawned on me, something I should have said a long time ago, perhaps, but here it is, anyway," she said, pouring him his drink. "Tom, you don't seem to be very happy to me. That young, dashing, adventurous man I once knew isn't here anymore. Oh yes, you're successful, many men would give their right arm to have what you've built up, but on the other hand, you're also not successful because you're not happy with what you have. That's how it looks to me every time I hand you a drink," she bravely told him. Tom remained silent as he took hold of the glass. "Why don't we try something, Tom?" Pat continued, watching her husband take a drink. "Why don't we go back to when we were starting out and start over?" she said.

He looked puzzled with a look she hadn't seen before. "I don't mean age-wise. I mean, why don't you start something new, something you'll have to work really hard on every day, say, a new business? Take ten thousand or so, maybe twenty thousand, and do something, buy something, make something. Just start over that way and let's see if you've still got it. It could be law, it could be anything, but it has to be something, Tom, or I'm afraid I'm going to lose you, Liz is going to lose you, and Emma is going to lose you," she challenged.

He took another drink and put the glass down and took a deep breath. "I'm not an alcoholic, Pat, if that's what you're thinking," he quietly protested. "I have this under control. But you're right, an old guy like me could use a new challenge now and again, and maybe things have been too easy, not enough to do, especially now that Liz has gone off to college. Maybe I can do more, a lot more, than just show up at the office. You're right, dear, maybe I can start something else and, who knows, go on to become a Rockefeller after all," he said, throwing his arms around her in a warm embrace and kissing her gently on the cheek.

Pat took a short step back. "That would be nice, but you don't have to become a Rockefeller to be happy either, Tom. Just take a look around you and you'll find plenty you can do, plenty of things, not only in business but also in day-to-day life," Pat responded, working up her courage. "Take a look around here, for instance, Tom. Take a look at the big picture, take a look at Emma. She's a big part of your life, and she wants you to pay attention to her and to be proud of her just as much as Elizabeth does. So please, Tom, give her some consideration. And just so you know, she's not doing as well with her grades as she could be. She's slipping some, and there's no reason for it other than what she's feeling inside. She's way too bright to be pulling just average marks," Pat continued while Emma quietly tiptoed her way to within a few feet from the doorway, unbeknownst to either of them.

Tom remained calm with his wife. "I'm going to take you up on the business idea, Pat, but Emma's your department. And I'm not going to send two daughters to Columbia when girl number two comes with an asterisk. No, Pat, Liz is going to finish at Columbia and then go to law school and then come into the practice. I've got more than enough on my plate with just her. Emma, on the other hand, is just going to have to live at home and go to a city college, and that's all there is to it," he said, reverting to his old, not-so-lovable self. Pat just shook her head in disgust.

"Tom, please, you've got to treat her more fairly. Can't you see what you're doing to her? It isn't right, Tom," she pleaded, but he wasn't dissuaded.

"I'm not doing it, Pat. I'm not sending her to Columbia or any Ivy League school for that matter. I'm not doing it, I'm not paying for it, and I'm not pushing her into law school. You've told me she's good at writing, so let her write. Let her become a writer or a secretary or whatever. It's not very important. I have made up my mind, and I'm putting it into Liz. I'm going to make not only a good lawyer out of her but also a good businessperson who can take over the firm from me when the time comes. Look, Emma's a good girl. She's smart, she's quiet, she's dependable maybe, but she's not the right type to handle any of the things concerning the firm, certainly not with me," he told her with a look of disdain.

Pat began to weaken. "Well, I can see—"

"You really don't see, Pat. How the hell do you think I've come this far with the business, anyway? By making judgments. I have to follow my gut instinct, and that includes whom I can work with and whom I can't. And I know I can't work with Emma on a lot of different levels. So there you've got it, right from the horse's mouth," he said just as Emma

41

slipped into the kitchen with a detached look on her face from trying to hide the emotions churning up inside.

"Mom, can I help you with anything before dinner?" she coyly asked.

"No, dear, just go sit down at the table, and your father and I will be in shortly," Pat replied, pretending as if nothing had happened at all.

Emma went into the dining room and sat down, trying to think how she would handle it. "How are things going, Father," she asked him, deciding it was not a good time to confront him.

Tom sat down and smiled, but he remained quiet while Pat brought out the food. "Anything new, Father, anything going on?" Emma probed while filling up her plate with another one of Pat's meticulously prepared dinners.

"Everything's fine, dear," Tom finally responded, seeming a little defensive.

Emma paused for a moment. "Everything's fine with me, too, I guess. But I do miss Liz, that's for sure," she muttered, trying to get him on topic.

"I'm sure you do, we all do," Pat added, sitting down at the table.

Emma saw an opening. "She must be doing great up there at Columbia, Father. I'll bet she really likes it," Emma declared.

Tom wasn't taking the bait. "Your mother says that your schoolwork has fallen off some, Emma. What's the story with that?" he asked, trying to appear more interested than he truly was.

"Yes, Emma, tell us, won't you? Why have your grades dipped?" Pat followed up.

Emma wasn't interested in explaining it to them. She began to eat, thinking of how to respond. In a moment, she had her answer. "Oh, it's nothing, really, Mom. And it's just one grade, not two or three or anything like that. I just had a little trouble with one of my teachers, my trigonometry teacher. She's got a foreign accent, and it's quite a bit difficult to understand her, so I didn't do too well on our first two tests. But the good news is, I'm getting more used to her, and I can understand her more now, so things should get better from now on," Emma explained.

Pat wasn't that convinced. "What if you aren't picking things up from her as good as you think you are?" Pat questioned with genuine interest.

"Oh, Mom, you know me. I can pick up my book anytime I want and nail it. Don't worry, Mother, I won't be needing a tutor the way Liz did to get into college. And you're not going to have to pull any strings for me either. I heard Father on the phone talking to them about getting her in. Nope, no tutor and no strings, that's just not going to happen because I won't be needing it," Emma confidently boasted, turning her head toward her father.

Tom took it as a really sassy remark. "You leave your sister out of it," he sternly warned her before continuing. "Now tell me more about how you are going to get yourself out of this fine mess you've gotten yourself into, Emma," he demanded.

Emma looked down at her plate, wishing he would only say something encouraging to her rather than just blow off more steam. But she couldn't think of anything to say without making matters worse, so she remained silent. Pat finally came to her daughter's defense. "Tom, Emma's already told you how she is handling the problem. She's going to go back to her plan B. She's going to study more instead of just attending class without picking up a book. That would be hard, even for you, Tom, to never have to study and just

43

depend on class time alone if you couldn't understand the teacher, like Emma's saying, dear," Pat protested.

Emma felt a profound sense of relief. "It's going to be all right, Father, really it is. I'll get through it. It's no big deal," she told him and then quickly finished her meal and left the table and went up to her room.

"I'm glad that's over with," Emma told herself, lying on her bed, propped up, trigonometry book in hand, thinking back to earlier in the evening. She was getting weary after two hours of reading. She put the book down on the night table and turned off the light. Then she looked up at the ceiling and saw the moonlight wash her room with its soft, tender radiance. She closed her eyes and began to review the episode between her and her father again. She felt alone and saddened by what she knew her relationship with him to be. Pat coming to her aid never entered her mind. All she saw and heard was Tom in the kitchen and Tom at the dinner table. She tried putting him out of her mind, and finally, she began to do so. For the first time, she found she could do it. She found she could replace him, for a brief time at least, by picturing the birth mother she had never known but had accidentally heard about as a child and conjuring her up to be the most wonderful person ever to walk on God's green earth. Emma saw her as a young, beautiful woman full of life and generous to a fault, with all the social graces, and intelligent—more intelligent than anyone she had ever known. Yes, Emma thought to herself in the glowing moonlight, this was her, this was her real mother, this was the stuff she herself was made of, and it felt wonderful, she thought, as she slowly fell off to sleep, longing to meet her.

VI

The sun shone brightly for a mid-September morning. Summer's heat had already given way to light, refreshing breezes as Liz, now a sophomore, walked briskly along the avenue of New York's Upper West Side neighborhood known as Morningside Heights, trying not to be late for her philosophy class. It was here that the proud Lions of Columbia had made their den, and it was here that Tom Molloy had graduated with honors from the law school those many years ago. Soon the storefronts and apartment buildings gave way to the ivory-tower excellence that hallmarked this university. Liz could feel the pressure. She picked up her pace and quickly glanced at her watch.

I can just about make it, she thought, pulling her books up that always seemed to be slipping out from under her left arm. She made her way up the broad, castle-like staircase and grabbed onto the mammoth door's handle, giving it her most powerful tug, just as the three books crashed to the ground. "Damn it," she shouted in disbelief before bending down to retrieve them. Resigned to the inevitable, Elizabeth slowly got down into a squat and was reaching for the first one when suddenly the large, almost mystical door opened by itself, as if by magic, and standing there before her was in her perception a very handsome young man who could have been one of the Greek gods for all she knew.

"Need a little help here, miss?" the young man calmly asked her, reaching down with his arm toward her books.

Liz took a deep breath. "Do you believe this?" she uttered, trying to maintain her composure.

He just smiled at her. "Here, let me," he confidently said, gathering up her volumes while she stood up next to him.

Liz smiled at him, trying to appear as though everything was just fine, but she was too anxious for the veneer to hold. "I've got to get to my class, Philosophy 101. I'm going to be late now that this had to happen," she lamented.

The young man chuckled, producing a bit of ire on Liz's face. "What's so funny?" she demanded, holding her ground with him.

"I'm coming from that very class myself. I'm in that class, but I haven't seen you there before. I wish I had," he gently added.

Liz seemed a bit confused at first, but then her demeanor lightened. "So what are you doing here then helping me if you should be in there?" she bantered, pointing to the great door.

"What's your name? I'm Steve Walsh," the man flirted, causing her to feel somewhat short of breath.

"You still haven't told me what you're doing here instead of sitting inside Philosophy 101, listening to Professor Winkman go on and on, expounding on the universal cause of the fall of man and other interesting topics like that," she joked, getting a laugh from her new admirer. "Is class cancelled?" she exclaimed.

Steve nodded his head. "You're in luck, my good lady. And you're very perceptive," he complimented, bringing a small smile to her face.

"That means I've got an hour and a half before my next class," she said with a sound of disappointment.

"We're in the same boat then," Steve replied, taking a couple of steps away from the building.

"Hey, where are you going with my books?" Liz playfully called to him.

Steve turned back and faced her, thinking she really looked beautiful standing there. "Well, you didn't tell me your name, so I don't know who to return these books to, these books here, the ones I just found lying there when you came along," he teased her.

Liz played along with him. "Well, Mr. Walsh, if that's the way it's got to be..."

"That's the way it's got to be," he tried persuading.

"Then let me tell you this, Mr. Walsh. I never give my name out to a stranger. But sometimes I might give it out to someone I've become acquainted with," she suggested.

Steve saw his opening. "We can go over to Frank's and get breakfast and, I dare say, get acquainted. That way, I'll know who I'm rolling my eyes to when Professor Winkman is up there, putting us all to sleep. Have you ever been to Frank's?" he continued, stepping back toward her and handing her two of her books.

"No, not Frank's," she answered.

Steve smiled at her. "Well, come on then. It's only a couple of blocks from here. We'll be back in plenty of time and still have time to maybe get acquainted," he said as they walked off together.

"Emma, is that you? I didn't hear you come in, dear," Pat called to her from the dining room, where she had been polishing the table.

"Yeah, it's me, Mother. I'm home, home from another boring day at Central College, Mother," Emma complained, tossing her book on the sofa and turning on the TV.

Pat walked over to her in the living room. "Don't be so glum, Emma. Central College is a fine school, and what's

47

nice about it is that it's so close to home. You can still be here while you're getting your education, not off in some dingy apartment, like Liz, with no one to look after you. Look at the bright side, dear. You've got all this home cooking, and you've got a friend here, Emma. I'm your friend," Pat sympathetically told her, trying to cheer her up but clearly seeing that it wasn't working.

"Mother, please leave me alone. I'm just a freshman there. I hate the place, and I'm condemned to three more years there after this one. So please let's talk a little reality here, Mother, for once if you don't mind. I'm not a kid, Mother, so please stop treating me like one," she argued.

Pat felt terrible. She knew that Emma had always been aware she had been treated differently, and now the thin cracks were obviously beginning to shatter. "Are you hungry, Em? Can I get you anything?" Pat asked, trying to change the subject.

"There you go again, Mother. No, I don't want anything—that is, anything to do with Central," she seethed.

Pat was beside herself. She turned and left the room and headed into the kitchen on the verge of tears, feeling guilty that she, too, was to blame for the unfair balance. But she knew she just didn't feel strong enough for it—no, she knew she just wasn't up to it; she couldn't take Tom head-on once more, only to have him screaming at her again and drinking more than before. A few minutes went by, and Pat regained her composure and went back to her daughter.

"Emma, I'm sorry I've let you down," she said, thinking of how she might tell her. Emma didn't say a word. Pat turned off the TV and sat down beside her but then nervously jumped to her feet again and walked over to the window. She looked out but couldn't see anything; she could only take a deep breath to cover her nerves. Then she finally turned toward her disgruntled daughter. "I'm going to tell you something, Emma, that I perhaps should have told you about many years ago but somehow didn't," Pat began, seeing on her daughter's face a sudden burst of interest.

"And what's that?" Emma responded, trying to seem as disinterested as possible.

"Emma, I'm going to tell you the truth about something that's important," Pat went on, now capturing her daughter's full attention.

"Go on, Mother," Emma prompted.

"Emma, my dear Emma, I'm not your mother in the way you've always believed. Emma, no, you're adopted," Pat confessed to her, scrutinizing her every move, searching for her true reaction. "That doesn't mean I'm not your mother. I am, but—and this is the only but to it—I'm not the one who brought you into this world."

"Like Liz." Emma interrupted, showing a flash of anger.

Pat took a second deep breath. "Yes, yes, Emma, that's right, like Liz," she owned up.

Emma leaned her head back on the sofa as a small tear rolled down the side of her face. "Then why are you telling me this now, today? Why today? Aren't parents like you supposed to break the big news flash several years ago or something?" Emma demanded. Pat couldn't answer her. "Aren't you supposed to prepare me for this long before I'm in college? And speaking of college, isn't this the reason it's good old Central for me but—and I mean it, Mother—it's Columbia for Liz? Because nothing is too good for Liz, right, Mother?" it poured out of her, while she tried holding back the tears.

Pat sat down beside her. "I suppose there is some truth to that with your father, Emma, but not with me. You are both equal in my eyes, but your father, well, it's perhaps a

49

little different with him. You see, before we got you, we lost a son, and it really affected him. Your father, like most men, I suppose, really wanted a son, and he was terribly disappointed when it happened—no, I take that back, he was out and out totally distraught. It completely changed him. To tell you the truth, Emma, he never really got over it. Don't think for a second that he would be doting over Liz had Tom lived, I don't think he would. But Tom didn't live, and he uses her to try to replace Tom in his own way," Pat tried explaining.

Emma wasn't really buying in. She felt the hurt even stronger as she kept thinking about Liz this and Liz that and Liz in Columbia, out on her own, really living and doing things, and herself a prisoner in this godforsaken house.

"What then is the solution, Mother?" Emma coyly asked, deciding not to tell her mother that she had overheard all of this a long time ago.

Pat tried to put her arm around her but then just began to cry. "You're right, Em, I should have told you earlier, much earlier, and I didn't. You have every right to hate me. I wouldn't blame you but I hope you don't," Pat pleaded in between the tears.

Emma's defenses were weakening at the sight of her mother crying next to her, and she thought about telling her that she already knew but decided to hold back. "I don't hate you, Mother, no, not at all. But I do hate Father. He may have had a hard time losing, Tom, you said his name was, but he didn't have to cripple me in the process. I used to have nothing but love for him, and all he ever did was ignore me. It was like I was never there, and it's really hurt me not just because that's how things are with him, but also because here I am, a lot smarter than Liz and a much better athlete, and I'm going nowhere in that poor excuse they call a college, and I walked out on track in high school, the best they had ever seen, because I felt like I just didn't fit in anywhere," she regretted.

"I know, Emma," Pat woefully agreed, looking straight into her eyes.

"So what then is the solution, Mother? I'll ask you one more time," Emma prodded, trying to gain an ally against her father.

Pat placed her hand on Emma's shoulder and slid over a little closer to her. "I'm not sure, not right now, Emma dear. But I can tell you this, from now on, I'm on your side, and I'll do whatever I can to reposition you with him, or maybe what I should say is, I'll do what I can to try to make it fairer around here for you. And that includes college and transfer-ring out of Central, I promise," Pat pledged to her, thinking only of rebuilding her trust before it was too late, if at all possible.

The head maître d' came up to him as soon as he arrived. "Good afternoon, Mr. Molloy, and welcome back to Le Chic. So nice to see you again, sir," he said, brimming with a smile.

"Nice to see you too, Tony," Tom replied.

"Will it be your usual table?" the smartly dressed man asked.

"Yes, I have a reservation," Tom told him.

"Ah why, yes, it slipped my mind. Come, please follow me, Mr. Molloy," he said, escorting Tom to one of the small tables in the rear by the window, overlooking a fine row of brownstone homes on the East Side's mid-sixties. "Shall I have something sent over from the bar, my compliments?" Tony asked, raising his hand in the air and snapping his fingers in the direction of one of the waiters who ran right over.

"Thank you, Tony. I'm expecting an important guest any minute. I'll order once he arrives," Tom said.

Tony looked at the waiter. "Take good care of my good friend here, Raphael, and the first round of drinks are on the house today," he told the young man, and the waiter promptly left them.

"That was very nice of you, Tony," Tom said, smiling up at a man he had known many years.

Tony leaned down and smiled back at him. "Enjoy your lunch, sir," he said and then he turned and walked away.

Tom looked at his watch. It was still early, he thought, starring out the window, observing the fashionably dressed people walking in the early autumn sunshine. One young, attractive, well-to-do-looking blond woman passed by, reminding him of Emma. Well, they looked somewhat alike, he thought, and they were about the same age. But no, this woman had more of an inner dignity, a self-confidence that seemed to say she knew what she was about, not at all like that bumbling daughter he had living at home. The parade on the street continued, and in a short time, Tom looked at his watch again and waved for Raphael to come over to his table.

"Let me have a scotch, ice—no, better, make that a double," Tom ordered, picking up his menu and pretending to read it.

"Right away, sir," the waiter answered and then quickly left him.

Tom recast his gaze back out onto the street, thinking about that beautiful woman he had just seen a few minutes earlier. If only Emma could be more like her, he was thinking to himself when suddenly a friendly voice that he recognized immediately called out to him.

"Tom, Tom, it's great to see you, old friend," his guest exclaimed with the happy look of two good friends coming together again.

Tom reached out his hand, and the two men shook as the elegantly dressed man, who was about Tom's age, sat down. "It's been too long, Brian," Tom said just as his drink arrived.

Toddman nodded his head in full agreement. "It's been about two years, I'd say. Boy, we sure showed them on that McManus case," Brian enthusiastically boasted.

Tom took a drink. "Raphael, see what my friend would like," Tom told him.

"Make mine a scotch and water, no ice," Brian told him, and then he turned his attention back to Tom. "So what did you want to see me about? No, let me guess, McManus came back and offered us stock options if we can keep his nose clean on this new waterpower project I've been reading about in the paper. What's he gotten himself into this time? Legally speaking, of course," Brian said as his drink showed up.

"We'll need a few minutes," Tom told the young man, and then he raised his glass and looked straight at his friend. "It's even better than that, Brian. This time, it's the Feds. They are making noises, no, they are already actually claiming that McManus Engineering is in breach, no, even worse, they're claiming fraudulent, deceptive practices on the Miller's Point nuclear power station, and from what I've been told, they have real evidence—evidence that will stand up in court," Tom revealed.

Brian raised his glass in the air next to Tom's. "Sounds serious, count me in," he said as both men clinked their glasses and took a drink. Brian put his glass down, put on his reading glasses, and picked up the menu. "This sort of thing sounds like it's going to be fun. I suppose you'll want to work it like we did the last time," he commented.

Tom took another drink. "Yeah, that's exactly what I had in mind," he said.

Brian looked over the menu. "Well, that sounds good to me, same terms on the fee, I suppose."

"Same terms," Tom responded.

Brian smiled a small smile and took a drink. "Well, now that that's over with, on with the important stuff. How's Pat and the kids? Elizabeth and Emma, right? How are they all doing?" Brian asked, making conversation.

Tom took a drink. "Pat's fine, and the girls are fine. And that's pretty good, you remembered both of their names," Tom said in jest.

Brian looked pleased. "Mine are both doing fine as well. Carol, my oldest, is heading off to Harvard, she's premed, and Gwen, two years younger, you might remember, well, Gwen, she takes after my side of the family even though, I've got to tell you, she's the adopted one. And she'll be going to either Fordham or maybe Yale and eventually go to law school. Either way, she's amazing, a chip off the old block," Brian confided as Raphael returned to take their order.

"Salmon for me with baked potato, sour cream, and peas. Don't let the chef undercook it, and bring over two more drinks," Tom said.

"Make mine fillet mignon, medium rare, and the rest just like his," Brian told him, handing him the menu and then looking back to his new business partner. "Yeah, Tom, I've really been blessed. I mean, things have worked out really well for Jennifer and myself—with our girls, that is. Carol was really the best thing that ever happened to us, so much so that we wanted another. When we discovered that Jen couldn't have a second child, we first figured what will be will be, like that song. That is, until Jen started feeling it and talked me into adopting. Well, anyway, I'm probably getting too carried away. I do have a few other interests I probably never told you about. And no, it's not golf. I gave that

54

damn game up last year finally. I joined a hunting lodge up in the Adirondacks. It's great fun, I met one of the guys I went to Fordham with. To be honest, we do more drinking than shooting, but it is kind of nice getting out in the country. Well, that's enough about me. I'll close my big trap. Tell me about you, Tom. How have the last couple of years treated you? Are your girls settled? Do they have things mapped out?" Brian asked.

Tom suddenly looked a little shaken, but he knew how to cover up well in these circles.

"What's wrong, old boy?" Brian casually asked him, sipping his drink.

"It's McManus, I guess. I was just thinking about the way the old man said it when he gave me the news. He seemed really nervous, much more so than last time, I thought. We're really going to have to roll up our sleeves on this one, Brian," Tom said, secretly wishing that his adopted daughter was more like Brian's, Gwen.

Brian agreed with him. "I'm with you all the way. Your gut feeling is correct, I'm sure of it, Tom. We'll do whatever it takes," Brian assured him.

Tom felt somewhat relieved. "How about I send the file over to your office later this afternoon?" Tom suggested.

Brian had been hoping for this. "Great, I'll take it home with me and read it over the weekend. That works out fine," he replied.

Tom could see that their waiter was heading toward them and that he appeared to be coming over to serve the meal. "Oh yeah, Brian, you mentioned something about my girls. Well, getting back to the girls, both Elizabeth and Emma are doing really fine," he told him just as their food appeared with the maître d' heading up the parade as if on cue.

"Bon appetite," Tony said proudly, saluting to Tom before walking away.

"He's a nice man. I'll have to remember to give him something at Christmas. Now let's eat, and then we can get on with our latest McManus adventure," Tom announced, hoping that the discussion about everybody's daughters had finally come to an end.

Later that afternoon, Liz arrived back at her small apartment a few blocks from the campus. The apartment was not too far from being nice, yet it was way too far from being large enough for any more than two, and two sometimes had trouble fitting into it.

"What are we doing tonight, Sally? Movies or studying, what's it going to be?" Liz nonchalantly asked her roommate, not really caring what her answer would be. Sally Winters was a very serious student with a precocious sense of humor.

"I say we stay in tonight and study. It's only Thursday after all," the tall attractive brunette told her. "Besides, Liz, you told me the other day how well you were doing, that you got your grades up from the beginning of the semester. Or was it that you got your grades up from the beginning of meeting a certain Steve Walsh? I can't remember which one it is. But no, it's in we stay and study, study, study so we can both enter the local little law school they've got around here, and we can both come out positively on top," Sally advised.

Liz laughed. "Somehow I already knew that would be your answer, Winters," Liz replied, placing her two books on the small desk on her side of the room.

Sally buried her head in the book she was reading. "So, Molloy, when am I going to meet this Mr. Walsh, anyway? When are you going to bring him up here? It'll cost you, you know, privacy, I mean, and I don't come cheap," Sally goaded her.

Liz wasn't taking any chances. "Not on your life, Winters. You'll only get to meet him after the ring gets on that little finger right there," Liz clawed back, waving her left hand under her roommate's nose.

Sally cracked up. "You know, Molloy, that's what I like about you. I… I like competing with you. If this Steve guy is even half as good as you claim he is, I wouldn't bring him around with me here either," Sally jabbed back.

Liz was unshaken. "Don't worry, I won't. I wouldn't want to interrupt even one precious minute or one precious second of your precious, all-encompassing studying time. Now as for tonight, what about getting some studying done before dinner, and then we'll figure out what we want to do later?" Liz suggested.

Sally had already made up her mind. "We'll stay in tonight and maybe catch a movie on the weekend—that is, if you're sticking around here then. Otherwise, there's always next week, but the main thing, Molloy, is what I just told you, that I wanted us both to get into the law school here. And I don't want any screwups, and that means boyfriend screwups also. Got it?" Sally commanded.

Liz took a deep breath. "Yeah, I've got it. But then that also applies to you when you finally dig up your own Steve Walsh. I'd like to hear you talk about life then, Miss Winters. You'll probably be more flipped out than I am over this guy—that is, if you would ever allow yourself more than five minutes out from under those books of yours," Liz reprimanded, holding back her own laugh, which was about ready to break through the surface.

Sally felt the urge to also laugh. "You've got a deal, Miss Molloy, touché. And now, if possible, will you please allow me to delve into the inner workings of Carlson versus Smithfield? And please let me know where you will be this weekend on the off chance that I will be able to tear myself away from Carlson and attend a fine film selection with you on Saturday," Sally proclaimed to her nearly bewildered friend.

It was midmorning that Saturday at the Molloy house. Tom was in the living room in his favorite wing chair by the front window, going over the McManus file. Things didn't look so good for poor old McManus, even with Brian Toddman on the case, he thought, putting his drink down on the end table.

"Don't forget, Tom, Liz will be over this morning," Pat called to him from the dining room. Tom didn't respond. "She may be bringing one of her girlfriends over from Columbia, so please be on your best behavior and don't spend all day with that...whatever it is you're working on. I thought we could take the girls out to lunch, maybe go over to The Grill or something like that. And, Tom, how about knocking off the liquor? It's a bit early even for you," Pat chided.

Tom took a sip of his drink and serenely leaned his head back and pictured Liz proudly striding down the aisle at her law school graduation with diploma in hand.

"Tom, did you even hear a word I said?" Pat interrupted, standing in front of him.

Tom looked up in a half-hearted manner. "Yeah, I heard you. Liz is coming, she's bringing someone, we're going out. See, there, I've got it, I am listening to you, Pat," he rejoined, watching as she turned around and left the room, giving him time for another viewing of Liz graduating from law school before he would be returning to McManus.

A few minutes went by, and Emma came running down the stairs. She passed by her father and headed straight into the kitchen, where Pat was at the sink cleaning up. "I'm going out, I'll be at Doris's for that study lesson I promised her," Emma stated, conveniently conjuring up a story for her mother to hear. Pat was very disappointed.

"But, Emma, I thought I told you... I know I told you that Liz is coming home today to spend the day with us," she bemoaned, handing Emma a dish towel. Emma handed it right back to her.

"You did, Mother, and you're right, I did say I would stick around for Queen Elizabeth's fabulous homecoming coronation. Nevertheless, I'm out of here. Doris is paying me one hundred dollars to show her how to do math, and I'm going over there. It's easy money, and that's all there is to it," Emma declared, turning to make her exit. Pat was beside herself.

"I don't think that's any way you should be talking about Liz. She's you sister, Emma, and it's just not right," Pat insisted, turning back to the sink while a small tear rolled down the side of her face.

"Mother, we've been over this, I'm going," Emma asserted, and she stormed out of the room toward the front door.

Tom glanced out the window and could see Liz coming by herself along the sidewalk toward the house. "What's with you, Emma? Where do you think you're going, young lady? Liz is here," he told her. Emma smirked at him but kept quiet as Tom got up and headed over to open the front door. "Hello, sweetheart, how's my girl?" he said to Liz as she entered the foyer, placing a kiss on her cheek.

"Hi, Daddy, I'm fine," Liz responded, putting her arms around him, giving him a big hug.

"It's so good to see you, it's great to have you back," Tom cheerfully exclaimed, escorting her into the living room.

Liz glanced over at Emma with something of a smile, a smile which seemed to indicate the victory over her that Liz felt inside. "And how are you doing, Emma? How have things been going around here for you," Liz asked in an almost disinterested fashion.

Emma recoiled within but kept her cool on the outside. "Things have been going great, Liz. As a matter of fact, I'm off now. I've got to give a tutoring lesson to someone in one of my classes. One of many who needs my help, I guess. She's a local girl, going to the local school. It's all very convenient. I'm so glad I don't have to schlep into the city the way you do," Emma countered, trying to remind her sister just who gave the tutoring lessons to whom. Tom wasn't amused.

"That's no way to act, Emma," he scolded, returning to his chair as Pat entered the room and walked up to her oldest daughter.

"It's so good to see you, dear," Pat said, giving her a big hug while Emma just rolled her eyes.

"It's great to see you also, Mother," Liz answered, returning the hug almost half-heartedly.

"So where is your friend, Sally, I think you said?" Pat asked her.

Liz nodded her head at her mother. "Yes, that's right, Sally. She's my roommate. She's a wonderful person. I'm very lucky to have her. But I must confess, she's serious to a fault, never without a book in her hand. No time for fun."

"So she's not coming?" Pat asked.

Liz shook her head. "No, she begged off at the last minute. So I just came by myself," Liz answered.

Tom smiled. "Well then, we have you all to ourselves, so much the better," he declared while Emma started for the front door.

"Great to see you, Liz. I'm sorry, but I've got to go. Catch you later," Emma told her and then she left.

Tom felt relieved. "I was just thinking of you before you got here, Liz. We need to talk about your future, your plans. We need to talk about you and see if you will one day be ready to join me at the firm," Tom said, returning to his file.

Liz felt excited. "Sure, Daddy. Why don't we have that talk in a little while after Mother and myself have a little girl-talk catching up to do?" she said in her friendliest manner as she and her mother left him and headed into the kitchen for what was sure to be one of Liz's best performances ever.

VII

The light snow had already stopped falling, barely covering the Molloys' front lawn. It was early evening, and the amber color from the streetlight glowed softly, almost dreamily, over the house. Several of the neighbors had outdoor holiday lights on this clear, cold Christmas Eve. Pat was in the kitchen with her last-minute preparations for the annual Molloy party, a small gathering of intimate friends and family, who customarily stopped by for a short time before heading out to the evening's various church services. This year seemed different to everybody. Perhaps it was because Liz had been away so long, perhaps it was because she was bringing a boy over to the house for the first time, but it did feel different somehow this year.

Emma was up in her room brushing out her long blond hair, grooming herself to look her very best, as the Molloys' front doorbell chimed.

"I'll get that," Emma anxiously called down to her parents as she darted down the stairs, excited at the prospect of seeing for the first time just who this Mr. Special was that her sister was bringing home for everyone to see. She made the landing and called out to her parents a second time, trying to keep them at bay, while she gathered herself with a deep breath and slowly opened the door for her sister and her date.

"Liz, you look terrific," Emma told her sister while looking over her beau.

"You look very nice too, Emma," Liz replied, dusting a little snow off Steve's shoulder.

"Did you have any trouble making it out from the city?" Emma asked, aptly noticing that this was a good-looking young man standing in front of her.

Liz was getting impatient with her. "Emma, this is Steve Walsh. Steve, this is my sister Emma," Liz said, getting the formal introductions over with as painlessly as possible.

Emma put out her right hand and shook his. "Nice to meet you, Steve. Liz has told us a lot about you," Emma invented as a gust of wind hit the door, causing Liz's flowered hat to blow off and land up against Emma's torso.

Liz reacted automatically. "Aren't you going to let us in? It's freezing standing here," Liz growled, grabbing the hat away from her sister and marching inside. Steve hesitated a moment and then followed behind her.

"It's very nice to meet you, Emma," he said, taking note that Liz's younger sister was a knockout.

Tom and Pat had already entered the living room. "Merry Christmas, Daddy," Liz said, heading over to her father with a big hug. Then Liz turned and hugged her mother. "Mom, Daddy, I want you to meet Steve Walsh. Steve is a friend of mine at school. He's the one I told you about, the one that I think would make a great lawyer someday," Liz bragged.

Tom's face lit up. "Welcome and Merry Christmas. Lawyers we like around here. We'll have to talk, but for now, come on in and make yourself comfortable," Tom said as the doorbell rang again. "Pat, see who that is, won't you?" Tom asked as he turned and headed over to the bar. Liz got out of her coat and hung it in the closet and then did the same with Steve's. Steve sat down on the sofa and was by now fixated on Emma, who stood before him. Emma returned his gaze with a glance while thinking that there had to be something wrong with this guy if he was even slightly interested in Liz. Steve broke the ice and made the first move.

"So Liz hasn't told me that much about you, Emma. Why don't you begin where Liz never really left off?" he asked, trying to sound both funny and sophisticated at the same time.

Emma wasn't impressed and just shrugged as Liz returned and sat next to Steve. "What's the latest at Central College? How are things going over there, Em?" Liz asked her, trying to actually look interested.

Emma paused and then sat down next to Steve. "My leg's been bothering me lately. I should probably go back to running," Emma answered, looking across at Liz and noticing that she was quickly losing interest.

"Yeah, how is Central? I heard it was a good school," Steve interjected in good spirit.

Emma felt a little flattered. "Things have been going all right. I'm a liberal arts student there. I seem to specialize in both writing and math, something of a dichotomy, one might say," Emma answered.

"I'm impressed," Steve responded as Pat came into the room to announce the arrival of her older sister.

"Liz, Em, come over and say hello to your aunt Doris. You haven't seen her in, oh, too long. It must be three years, I'm afraid," Pat lamented. The nicely dressed and obviously wealthy older woman smiled at them both.

"Don't bother getting up, Liz, Emma. I'll just come over and give a big hug to you," she said, bending over and throwing her arms around each of them, nearly tripping over Steve as she made her way.

"Come, Doris, say hello to Tom," Pat said to her, and the two women left.

Liz was exacerbated. "That was close, Steve. You nearly had the Hindenburg crash-land on your lap," she sniped.

Emma laughed. "Yeah, we have a few of those over at Central," she rejoined, trying to refocus the conversation back on her. Steve took the bait.

"So, which is it, Emma?"

"Which is what?" Emma countered.

"Writing or math, which do you like better and which are you better at?" Steve asked.

"Oh, she's always been writing her stories," Liz jumped in.

Emma nodded. "Yeah, that's true, but to tell you the truth, I'm probably better at math and like it more, but the writing does offer a chance to escape, to never be alone."

"How so?" Steve questioned, looking straight into her soft blue eyes.

"Well, you see, whenever I write a story, I get to know my characters really well. It's like they're alive, and some I like and some I don't like, but at least they are always there for me, and I find that interesting and nice," Emma explained.

Steve couldn't take his eyes off her. "I find that interesting also. I mean, it really makes sense," he praised her, feeling a tug on the arm from Liz.

"Come on, Steve, let's get a drink, and then we can go over and talk to Daddy. He wants to do a little lawyer-to-prospective-lawyer cheerleading, so let's keep him happy," Liz directed, rising to her feet.

Steve paused. "It's been really nice to meet you, Emma. I hope to see you again. And keep up with your writing. You never know," he told her, rising to his feet to leave with Liz.

Emma felt really good about herself, hearing his compliments. Perhaps Liz might have found something here, she thought to herself.

It was the first day of back-to-school week at Columbia following that year's Christmas and New Year's break. For Liz, it was becoming more of a routine that she found herself to be good at. The New Year's party she went to with Steve had been a raving success in her mind, and she found herself to be in genuinely good spirits as she left the campus to join Sally Winters over at Frank's Restaurant for some catching up between friends. The late afternoon was turning dark quickly as Liz made the trek over to the college hangout, fully anticipating the envious reaction she was about to receive. Liz walked in and saw that the place was almost empty and that Sally had yet to arrive. A portly middle-aged man with a friendly smile greeted her as she entered.

"Hi, I'm Joe. Where would you like to sit? Would you like a booth?"

"A booth in the rear, that will be fine," Liz told him and followed him over to a nice table where she could see who would be coming in. "How come your name isn't Frank?" Liz asked him, placing her books down, trying to pass the time.

The man chuckled. "Everyone asks me that. I bought the place from Frank. He's my brother-in-law, and I guess I just never got around to changing the name. I figured the delivery guys would never find it," he joked with her good-naturedly.

Liz was getting tired of him. "I'm waiting for a friend, I'll order when she gets here," Liz blurted out. Joe placed two menus on the table before her and turned and left. Liz began thinking about the party she went to on New Year's and how Steve had told her that he liked her father and had a really good talk with him about law and the firm and the possibilities that may present themselves in the future. Off to a very good start, she confidently told herself as Sally walked over with another girl whom Liz didn't recognize.

"Hi, Liz, this is Joan McCarthy. We sit together in Professor Crowley's dreadful English class, English for the walking dead. We're two long-suffering souls waiting for that dribble to end," Sally said as the girls both sat opposite Liz, who felt pretty disappointed that Sally had brought her along. Joe came right over with a third menu, directly on Liz's radar.

"We need a little time, Joe," she impatiently told him, chasing him off. Sally looked over at her roommate with a big smile.

"I know what I want. I want to hear how you made out with lover boy at your family Christmas party," Sally bluntly stated. Liz was ready for her.

"You might say that it went very well, thank you," she replied in her most proper-sounding Queen's English.

"Go on," Sally prodded, picking up her menu, trying to appear somewhat detached.

"We had a real nice time. Steve met my father, and they seemed to hit it off all right. My father told me that he was impressed with Steve and that he probably would make a good lawyer someday," Liz continued. Sally dropped her menu on the table.

"That's not exactly what I'm talking about, Liz," Sally said, jabbing her friend next to her with her elbow. Liz seemed a bit off-center.

"And he met my aunt and my sister, and things went very well, actually," Liz told her. Sally kept it up.

"She's just not getting it, Joan," Sally told her. Liz quickly perked up.

"Oh, you mean, did he give me a ring yet?" Liz asked her. Sally began to smile, but it quickly became a laugh.

"We're not talking about rings on your finger and buttons and bows, silly. Did he sleep with you?" Sally blurted out, much to Liz's astonishment. Joan saw the look on her face and tried to smooth things over.

"Don't be embarrassed on my account, Liz. I've slept with a couple of boys, it's no big deal as long as you're careful," she confided. Sally joined in behind her.

"Joan's right, it is just that, no big deal. This isn't the Dark Ages for crying out loud. So did you, or didn't you? We all have inquiring minds at this table, or we shouldn't be attending a school like this in the first place," Sally rationalized. Joan returned to Sally's position.

"Go on, Liz, it's just us girls here. Besides, it's a hell of a lot more interesting than debating Winters over here on the merits of Carlson versus Smithfield. I'm going to go to law school also, but every now and again, even I've got to drop it for a while and have some fun," Joan coaxed, trying to lay the groundwork for some full disclosure.

Liz wasn't buying into it. She could feel the tug of her Catholic school roots pulling on her more than she would ever have expected. "Well, to tell you both the truth, I'm a virgin and I feel that it's nothing to be ashamed about. In fact, I'm rather proud of it and plan to stay that way until I get married," she asserted in a slightly condescending tone.

Joan looked toward Sally. "I think we should be ordering. I've got to go soon, I've just thought of something I need to do," she begged off. Sally wasn't giving up so easily.

"Well, just because you're a virgin, it doesn't make you any better than anyone else. And with what you've told me about Steve, you could be lying, but no, I suppose you're too prudish to be lying in the first place. But get ready for it because most guys aren't going to wait around forever," Sally sternly imparted to her.

Liz looked up at the ceiling and rolled her eyes. "So I take it you're not, Sally," Liz provoked, turning the tables.

"No, I'm not. I'm liberated from all that stuff. I'm not going to let some old-fashioned, social gobbledygook tell me how I have to live my life. It's really simple," Sally retorted, returning to her menu.

Liz pushed on. "Then it's settled, to each his own—I mean her own—and we can now get on with everything else," she declared just as Joe came back over to take their order and just as Joan got up to leave.

A few days later, Central College opened its doors and dusted itself off from the winter's holiday break. The city bus pulled up on Kingsley Boulevard to let most of its passengers off on the other side of the street, opposite the front entrance to the school. Steve Walsh was sitting in his shiny, brand-new black Corvette a dozen feet or so behind the bus stop in perfect position to see just who got off. A small crowd of young people had accumulated, waiting for the bus to pull away. And then Steve spotted her, the one girl he couldn't stop thinking about. He quickly exited his vehicle and started toward her.

She didn't see him as he approached behind her. The bus pulled away, and the students began crossing the busy street in unison, some chatting with each other but most were focused on their own thoughts and the buildings that lay before them in the cold morning air. When the group had practically all crossed the boulevard, Steve saw his chance and quickly closed in on her, trying to hold his nerve. He reached out and tapped her on the shoulder with a gentle smile across his face.

"Haven't we met somewhere before?" he glibly asked her.

Emma turned around and saw that it was Steve. "What are you doing here?" she asked him, looking somewhat confused.

Steve forced a slight chuckle. "I'm here on a mission of mercy, Emma, and you're the only one who can help me," he invented as she turned back to face the school. Steve took a step forward. "You see, my kid sister is in high school, and she isn't really sure of what she wants to do, you know, what school, what career and all that," he told her as they began walking together.

Emma was still really surprised to see him. "So how does that explain—"

"Explain my being here? Yes, well, that one's easy. You see, from where we live over in Malba, this would be the perfect place for Mary to go. If she wanted to continue, she could transfer on, and if she wanted to, say, just do a couple of years, well, that would be all right too," he explained.

Emma was really impressed by his loyalty to his sister. "That's really sweet of you to think of her like that, Steve," she said as they headed up the asphalt path toward Emma's first class.

Steve felt a little emboldened. "Mary does have something of a learning disability, she's a little slow when it comes to math, but other than that, she's fine," he added, trying to gain her sympathy.

Emma began to feel suspicious of his story and started to wonder how he just happened to appear the moment she got off the bus. "So tell me, how on earth did you manage to bump into me like this? I mean with the bus and all. It couldn't have been by coincidence," she questioned.

Steve knew he'd have to come clean. "Well, Emma, it's like this. I contacted the transit authority and got the Queens bus schedule and figured you'd be starting class in the neighborhood of right about now, and then I just went for it, got a good parking space, saw you, met you, and here we are. Now just so long as my car doesn't get stolen, I'd say we're in pretty good shape," he bantered along, seeing a small smile light up on her beautiful face.

"So you weren't stalking me then," she lightheartedly quipped.

"Well, not really, but I did need to see you. You're the only person I know who has anything to do with this place, and the part about Mary is true, honest," he said, trying his best to convince her.

Emma wasn't sure if she should believe him, but she didn't want to offend him either. No, he could prove to be more useful as an ally, she reasoned. "Well, I do know where the administration building is. That's it over there. I suppose you could pick up all of the forms you might need for her over there with them," Emma suggested as they approached her destination.

Steve stopped and put his hand on her shoulder, turning her to face him. "Thanks for your help," he nervously told her, wondering what to say next.

Emma filled in the blank space. "I'm going to be out in one hour. If you're still here by then, if you want to go over anything or ask me any questions about Central College, well, I'll be here, and I'd be more than happy to help you, Steve," she proposed without the thought of Elizabeth even entering her mind.

Steve was both relieved and happy at the same time. "I'll probably still be stuck in there with them for about that much time. What do you say we meet over there? That bench will be good," he hopefully answered, glancing down at his watch.

Emma was also happy. "Okay then, Steve, ten o'clock it is at the bench," she said, turning away from him and heading off to class.

Steve left and headed over to the administration building. The directory there indicated he needed to go to the second floor for prospective student services. He took the staircase up and entered the office and took a number and sat down to wait to be called. Steve closed his eyes and imagined Emma's face smiling at him in a sultry, seductive manner. He envisioned her alone with him, pleading with him to never leave her, lying beside him in the best suite at the Waldorf. Yes, this was the girl, a girl he wanted more than any other girl he had known before. He could almost feel the softness of her long blond hair in his mind, and pictured her out on the ski slopes with him and proudly parading his trophy around the lodge in front of his buddies.

Suddenly, a matronly, middle-aged woman came over to him, rudely knocking him out of his fantasy. "What can I do for you, sir?" she asked in a semirobotic way.

"I'm here to pick up some of the basics for admission to your school," Steve respectively answered.

The woman seemed somewhat annoyed. "When you say basics, what exactly do you mean?" she curtly replied.

Steve felt his heart race a little. "I'm interested in admission. Can you provide me with the forms, or do I need to speak with someone else?" Steve said with a frustrated look on his face.

The woman took a step closer. "Young man, I'll need more to go on. What course of study do you plan to pursue? What are you intending to do after you graduate? Are you going to go on and get your four-year degree at another institution? And if so, what will that be? You, like so many others, come into this office ill-prepared, and it's my job to ensure that you take the necessary time and give it the necessary thought to make an intelligent decision," she expounded, lavishing herself in her own air of superiority.

Steve was getting really tired of her, but he knew he had to have some plausible forms in his hand when he met back with Emma. "Yes, ma'am, you're absolutely right. I do need to supply you with whatever it is you're talking about for my slightly disabled sister, for whom this exercise is all about. You see, miss... I didn't get your name."

"Emerson."

"Yes, Ms. Emerson. You see, Ms. Emerson, Mary, that's her name, well, she's in high school and she doesn't drive. We live in Malba, and, well, I had some other business around here, so here I am, doing that proverbial good deed that never goes unpunished."

Emerson seemed to soften a little with his story. "Well then..."

"Steve, Steve Walsh."

"Well then, wait here, and I'll get you some general information about admissions and some of our programs, including financial aid," she said.

"Oh, the financial aid part won't be necessary," Steve said, hoping she would just get on with it.

The woman smirked a bit. "Lucky you," she coarsely said under her breath.

Steve glanced at his watch. "Is there anything else you might need to know?" he cautiously asked her.

The woman's face brightened. "Tell me, Mr. Walsh, you said something about your sister being slightly disabled. Could you tell me something about that? What type of disability are we talking about here? Is she in a wheelchair? What are we talking about?" Emerson questioned.

Steve was beginning to lose his patience. "No, it's nothing like that. She has a little trouble with math, she's slow at math, that's all. And from what I can see around here, that won't be a problem. She'll probably go to the head of the class in this place," he fired at her.

Emerson's face got beet red. "Well, I've never in all my years here—"

"And it looks like there have been too many of those," Steve jabbed her.

"In all my years, I've never—"

"Lady, who the hell cares? Just do your job and get me some of your dam forms, please. I've really got more important things to do than carry on this conversation," he blurted out while looking down at his watch again.

Emerson quickly turned and walked off in a huff, while Steve took a deep breath to try to calm himself down before going back to picturing Emma in his arms again.

It was a few minutes past ten when Emma reached the bench Steve had asked her to meet him at. The sun was out, and Emma was genuinely feeling good about the meeting that was about to take place. She was a bit surprised to be the first one there because she really didn't know what to believe about Steve's so-called errand of mercy for Mary. She sat down and leaned her head back and began daydreaming into the beautiful blue sky. She closed her eyes and pictured her sister Elizabeth in her mind. What a way to make her pay, just steal her boyfriend and then let her know about it. A smile lit up across her face. It almost seemed too good to be true, like winning the grand prize.

She opened her eyes and saw a young couple strolling across the courtyard about twenty yards from where she was sitting. They looked so happy walking arm in arm together, talking and laughing as they went past her. No, this would never do, she thought, not for her and Steve in spite of Elizabeth. No, Emma decided, she wasn't going to play the "steal your boyfriend" card on her sister. If things ever did really work out between her and Steve, she told herself that she would cross that bridge once she got there, but for now, no, way too early, she thought as Steve approached her from the direction of the administration building.

He didn't look very happy; maybe there was something to his "help my little sister" story after all, Emma thought. She could see that he hadn't spotted her yet. She looked back over to the young couple again, who by now were fading in the distance. "No, Elizabeth, today's your lucky day," she muttered to herself as Steve first took sight of her.

"Sorry I'm late. You wouldn't believe what they've got working up there. I felt like I was dealing with the last remaining member of caveman one-o-one, but I did get all the necessary forms for Mary, and now that that's all done, I can place my full attention on you," he said, sitting down beside her.

Emma inched back from him. "So what do you want to talk about?" she quietly asked him. There was a moment of silence.

"Nice day out," Steve nervously stammered, not knowing where to go next. Emma filled in the blank.

"Steve, let's be frank with each other. I like you. You're a real nice guy, and who knows, maybe I could even someday more than just like you. But—and here is a very big but—in case you've forgotten, you're my sister's boyfriend, and I don't think—"

"You don't think what?" Steve interrupted.

Emma was somewhat surprised at his assertiveness. "Well, I don't know. Maybe I'm just imagining—"

"Imagining what?" he countered. Emma began to blush.

"Steve, you're making this very difficult for me, so please just listen. I'm—"

"You're going to tell me to lay off because of Liz. Understood. You're going to tell me that we shouldn't be seen together."

"No, not exactly," Emma interjected.

Steve took a deep breath to try to relieve the tension. "Emma, then will you please tell me exactly what it is that you're telling me?" he exclaimed.

Emma burst out laughing. "Oh, Steve, you idiot. All I'm really telling you is that we can be friends, we can be seen, but we can't be like them over there," she said, pointing to another young couple passing by.

Steve had expected this all along and was ready for her. "Well, Miss Overrated, now that we've cleared the air, or should I say you've cleared the air, let me tell you that I really just came by to pay a visit to someone I thought would make a good friend. I really care about your sister, and so far, I still think I like you, so let me take back Miss Overrated and let me apply Miss Emma to that instead," he said, putting up the best front he could come up with.

Emma inched herself back a little more and smiled at him. "Well, that's good to know," she said in her most innocent little girl voice.

Steve wasn't entirely giving up. "So let me just add, friend to friend, that as a friend, if there's ever anything I can do to help you someday, let me know. It's what I do. I help people. Today, it's my sister Mary. Two weeks ago, I got my neighbor's cat out of their tree, and let me tell you something, that was some tree, over forty feet tall. And next week, well, who knows, I could be on the evening news for something or other," he joked, trying to keep her in the game.

76

Emma thought for a moment, and then she saw her opening, an opening to something she had wanted for a long time. "Well, that's awfully terrific of you, Steve, or should I call you Saint Stephen. But there is one thing you could do for me," she playfully remarked.

Steve felt his heart race. "And what might that be, Miss Emma, my friend?" he asked her.

Emma took a moment before answering; she wanted to be careful with this one. "You've got to promise me as a friend—no, you've got to swear on the grave of Saint Stephan that you will never tell a soul anything about what I'm going to tell you. Anything, do you swear?" she demanded, sounding like a harsh, even callous version of herself.

Steve became visibly upset with her ultimatum, but he just couldn't walk away. "You've got me, Saint Stephan swears," he said soberly, looking her straight in the eye.

For Emma that wasn't good enough. "No, Steve, you're not getting it. No kidding around here. I'm very serious. You've got to really swear, you, not some phony pledge you're inventing from a saint. No, Steve, it's got to be you doing the swearing," she insisted.

Steve was too intrigued to turn her down. "Okay, Emma, you win. I swear that anything you say or anything that we talk about here and now will never be repeated by me. You've got my word, I swear. What else do you want?" he demanded, becoming somewhat annoyed with her.

Emma nodded at him. "Okay, Steve, it goes like this. Do you know how sometimes things just aren't the way they seem to be? Well, that's how it is with me. You see Elizabeth and me and you think to yourself, oh, that's nice, they're sisters, and that's how it should be and life goes on. But that's not how it is. We're not sisters, not really, you see, because I'm adopted and she's not. She's theirs, I'm someone else's, and oh boy, do they…do they ever let me know it, especially—my quote—father. He really lets me know it, he has for years.

"So, Steve, now that the cat's out of the bag, here is what I'm asking you for. I'm asking you for some help. I'm asking you to help me find my birth mother. I know all about your family, well, maybe not all about but a lot about your family and their connections to people in high places. Liz and I do talk every now and again, if you can believe that, and whenever we do, she's usually bragging to me about something, and with you in the picture, her bragging rights just went up by a factor of twenty," Emma divulged.

Steve was conflicted. He felt he could gain the advantage with her here, but at the same time, after seeing her bare her soul, he wanted to actually help her. "I can't promise you anything in terms of getting you the desired result, but I'm more than happy to give it a try. And yes, my family is pretty well connected to some pretty important people," he told her in a reassuring manner.

Emma felt a sense of relief. "I've tried contacting agencies, but it's just no good. I can't get anywhere with them. I've even gone to one in the city, and the woman there said that even if I presented her with all the necessary information, she couldn't help me. State law, they won't allow it. They won't disclose anything, especially if you're in my age bracket," Emma lamented, inching her way a little closer to him.

Steve slowly got up from the bench. He reached into his wallet and pulled out a business card and handed it to her. "Call me, Emma, after you put together a dossier on your story. Have it include any names you can think of, names of people, names of institutions, names of anything. When you call me with it, I'll tell you where to send it, and I'll take it from there. I have two, maybe three people who come to mind who can cut through all the baloney and get to the answer, get you the truth. Trust me, Emma, these people are heavyweights. They can get past any piddling agency, or state law, for that matter," Steve boldly asserted.

Emma felt hopeful for the first time in a long while. She got up and took hold of his hand. "I think you already know what this means to me, so I'm not going to say anything other than thank you, Steve. Thank you so very much," she said and she turned and walked back to the classroom building she had been in a little while before, leaving the young man standing there, a young man who was both very hopeful and very eager for their next encounter.

VIII

––––––––

Several weeks went by, and the late-autumn, early-winter blue skies in Flushing were just a faded memory that had already given way to the colder, darker, more threatening grays that ultimately would dominate the remaining winter. Patricia had been doing her usual things at the Molloys' home. Nothing had really changed that much for her at all, except for one thing, and that one thing is what turned Emma's life upside down.

"You can go in and see her now, Emma. You've been wonderful coming to visit her so often. It really means a lot to patients. I've been here at Queens Memorial Hospital for over ten years, and I just wish that others would find the time the way you have," the tall nurse at the desk told her.

Emma got up from the chair and walked into the room. It didn't look too good. Her mother lay on the bed before her, barely conscious, connected to wires and tubes running everywhere, following the massive heart attack and ensuing operation. Pat slowly opened her eyes and spotted her daughter standing there. She motioned with her arm for Emma to come closer.

"I'm not doing so good, am I?" Pat asked in a little more than a whisper.

Emma tried holding back the tears as she gently took hold of her mother's hand. She forced a smile and began to cry. "Mother, I love you very much, you know that. I don't want you to talk like that, please don't. You're going to get through this. We're all praying for you, and you're going to get through this," Emma encouraged her, bending over to place a kiss on her cheek just as the tall nurse entered the room.

"All right now, Mrs. Molloy, look what I have for you. Only one blue pill this time. You must be doing something right," the nurse said while she placed her tray on the table and the blue pill carefully in Pat's mouth. "Now just bear with me a second here, and you'll have your water to wash it down. The medication will help you sleep, and it's a great painkiller. I know, I use it whenever my husband gives me a headache, which is quite often, I might add," she said, trying to cheer up Pat. The nurse then removed the glass from Pat's lips, picked up her tray, and turned and left them together.

Emma walked around to the other side of the bed. "I'm doing really well over at Central, Mom. I've been selected by the head of the English department to go into this advanced writing program they've set up. The dean himself came into the class and told us we should all go on to become writers, that we were specially selected. They only have five students in the whole thing, so I guess that means I must be pretty good at it, don't you think, Mom?" Emma tearfully told her.

Pat's face lit up a bit at the good news. "I always knew you had talent, Emma. Now go and use it and know that you can do anything you set your mind on," she slowly said, squeezing onto her daughter's hand before dozing off back to sleep for the last time in her life.

The long, slow procession entered All Saints Cemetery in a single file. The dark, gray sunlight just barely shone through, and the wind was beginning to pick up quite a bit from the time they had left the church. The pastor at St. Rita's, Father Bob, had given a very respectful eulogy. He had known Patricia in a cursory manner over the years, not really knowing her but always there with a quick smile whenever their paths crossed and always there to encourage her to get more involved in the parish and some of its various functions. It seemed to many at the service that he was particularly generous in talking about Pat's contributions, for nearly everyone there knew she embodied the prototypical stay-at-home wife of the period.

It was a short ride back to the Red Fox restaurant, where the family gathering was to take place, just a few blocks from the Molloy home. Emma had already arrived when Liz walked in with her boyfriend, Steve. They both sat down opposite Emma, who had taken a table toward the back.

"How's Father holding up?" Liz asked her sister while getting out of her coat.

Emma didn't bother to look up. "As good as one could expect, I suppose."

"It's going to take time, Emma. He's going to have to be strong, and he will be strong, if I know him. Look, the man built a business, that shows you something. He's strong. He's going to be okay. Just a little time, that's all," Liz said, almost sounding like an authority on the subject.

"How are you doing, Emma?" Steve asked her, taking Liz's coat from her to go and hang up. Emma didn't answer him but rather looked away, so he left them.

"You surely didn't overburden yourself visiting Mother in the hospital. What the hell were you thinking? That she was just going to unplug herself from the wall and walk home? You've got to be kidding, Liz. I mean, her nurse up there told me you didn't even come to visit her once. Too busy at school or too busy trying to tie down Mr. Right over there?" Emma scolded.

Liz wasn't in the mood for her younger sister's sarcasm. "Who the hell do you think you are, anyway, Miss Righteous, Miss I Don't Know What? You've got to be kidding me. I was always closer to her than you ever were. I mean, all those years, I was the one who spent more time with her when we were growing up. You were always up in your room sulking about something to have much time for Mother, and believe me she knew it too," Liz fired at her as the room was steadily filling up with mostly guests who were friends of the family.

Emma could see that Steve was up at the bar having a drink. "You know, you little bitch, that you're not going to land him. You'll never get him to marry you. It will never happen," Emma flatly stated.

Liz stared her down with daggers. "And what the hell are you lying about now? What do you even know about me and Steve, or anything, for that matter?" Liz challenged as an old waiter appeared next to them. "Not now. Go away," Liz ordered the old man before turning her attention back on her sister.

Emma let her have it. "I know that he followed me to school one morning. He accidentally on purpose just happened to bump into me at Central a couple of months or so ago, and he certainly wasn't there to tell me how much he adored you. Trust me on that one," Emma triumphantly announced.

Liz's face began to glow red. "You're lying. He wouldn't even set foot on that dump you call a campus. Besides, you've always had your fabulous imagination. You're liable to make anything up, even something as preposterous as this," Liz retaliated.

Emma stuck the knife in deeper. "Then why don't you ask him? Go on, ask him. Or would you like me to bring it up when he gets back over here?" Emma threatened.

Liz began to believe that Emma was possibly telling her the truth, but she wasn't about to give in. "I'm going over to Father, you little liar. We'll just see how big a liar you are later," she said, getting up and retreating from the table.

Emma felt relieved that the battle was over—for the time being, anyway. She sat there gazing around the room, thinking back to her last meeting with her mother at the hospital a short time before and knowing now that from now on, it would be war with Liz.

Steve looked over from the bar and saw Emma sitting by herself. "What can I get for you?" he casually asked her as he approached her table, drink in hand. Emma looked up and smiled. She reached into her purse and pulled out a small envelope, a blank slip of paper, and a pen and handed it to him.

"Don't open it here, Steve, and jot down your phone number. The envelope contains that dossier you told me to construct at Central that day. The one you said to get for you. And remember, not a word, just like you promised," she told him.

"I'm sorry about your mother," Steve quietly said, taking the envelope from her and putting it inside his jacket pocket.

Emma was touched. "She meant a great deal to me. You know, it's funny, all those years and she never told me much. She never told me anything in the way of encouragement or anything like that, but wouldn't you know it? There, on what was to be her deathbed, there, at least, she told me I had talent. She told me to go for it. I suppose it's something she was wishing she had done in her life," Emma poignantly confided.

Steve had a sympathetic look on his face as he pulled the chair back to sit down opposite her. He looked around the room and quickly wrote down his number and handed her back the paper with the pen. "She's right, you know, your mother, that is. One should go for it if one has talent, and it certainly sounds like you just might be one of those lucky people. I think you should go for it, Emma," he encouraged just as Liz returned and stood next to the table.

"Well, I see you two are getting along nicely. Steve, you'll have to excuse us, but we need to go over and see my father, together. Come on, Em, he's pretty bad and he wants to see us both. Right now," she insisted, grabbing Emma by the arm and giving her a strong tug. "Right now, he's waiting," Liz repeated.

Emma slowly rose to her feet. "It's nice to see you again, Steve," Emma said, and she turned and followed Liz across the room out into the hall toward a small room. "How bad is he?" Emma asked.

Liz was as distant as ever. "Don't push him too much about his drinking, he needs something, especially today," she ordered.

Emma became angry with her, but she didn't want a repeat of their earlier scene. "I won't if you won't," Emma promised. "Besides, I never really got on his case about it at all anyway. In any event, I won't say anything this time, but I will tell you that I am concerned. I'm the one who's still living there not you," she said with something more than just a slight sense of trepidation.

The two women entered the closed-off section of the restaurant and saw their father sitting alone at a table. "Hi, Daddy, here she is," Liz said, sitting down.

"How are you, Father?" Emma asked as she sat down.

Tom had more than a sullen look on his face. He looked like he was seriously in a state of depression. "I'm all right, Emma," he drew the strength to say. Emma remained silent, hoping he would continue. Tom sternly glanced across the table at her. "But, Emma, something does concern me, something your mother and I talked about more than once, and this is it. I'm concerned about how you two girls get along. I'm concerned because we're a family, and I know that you two aren't, shall we say, very close. And I'm concerned about the way you've treated Liz here today. She came to me before with tears in her eyes. She told me about your story, your story with Steve. Now I want this bickering to stop right now. I'm having a hard-enough time going through losing your mother. I don't want to lose my entire family. You don't have to pretend to be best of friends, but you do have to be civil to each other, especially when I'm around. Is anybody not getting any of this?" he continued.

Emma felt as though she had been ambushed once again, but her sorrow for his loss was even stronger. "All right, Dad, it's a new beginning. I'm in," Emma sincerely told him.

"And are you in also, Liz?" Tom asked her.

Elizabeth took a deep breath. "Father, you know I'm in. I don't want all this fighting. I don't start fights. I don't want any part of them, unless I become a lawyer, that is, and do some good fighting for the firm. But family-wise, I don't want any fighting, and there won't be any, provided she doesn't lie to me and she doesn't go around trying to steal what is mine. And that means my boyfriend," Liz blurted out, staring directly at her sister.

Tom was shocked at Liz's allegations. He thought for a moment and then he slowly got up from the table. "Emma, if this is true, you've got to stop it at once. And, Liz, if this is not true, you've got to do a lot better. And I will tell you one other thing. Emma, I won't have any lying, stealing, or any of that in my house," he angrily stated and then he walked out of the room.

Liz felt relieved inside. She pushed her chair back and faced her sister. "Well, I think you get the picture. So if Steve does make a play for you, I want you to understand something. I'm not going to give him up so fast. I'll get him back from you, I swear I will, no matter what it takes. Remember that, Emma. And remember this. Our father just called you out, not me, in case you weren't paying attention. So here's the deal; you make me unhappy, I'll make your life miserable," she threatened and she got up and stormed out of the room.

IX

About a week went by, and the front doorbell rang at the Molloys' house. Emma quickly came out from the kitchen through the living room to the front door and opened it. There standing before her was her father, Tom, still fumbling for his keys and obviously feeling no pain.

"Couldn't get them out of my pocket. What's for dinner, Emma?" he said, stammering through the foyer. Emma just rolled her eyes as he passed in front of her. This was the third time this week he came home after he had been drinking. Tom walked over and threw his coat on the sofa and slumped into one of the cushions.

"What's for dinner, Emma?" he asked her again. Emma was really frustrated.

"Hamburger, we're having hamburger. It's about the only thing I have time for. I do go to school, too, you know," she exclaimed.

Tom started to laugh to himself. "You know, Emma, maybe you shouldn't bother going to school so much. We've already got one genius in the family, and she's already committed to taking up the law. I don't hear anything like that coming out of you. All you ever talk about when you're so inclined is writing. What the hell is that going to get you other than broke? You should be trying to come up with something other than your stupid writing. Writing stories or whatever you call them is a sheer waste of time. Nobody is going to pay you to do that. Trust me. Now, on the other hand, if you took your fabulous writing and applied it to the law, then you may have something, something you can get paid for," he droned on, pulling himself up and making his way into the kitchen to make a drink.

Emma became alarmed. "How do they look?" she nervously asked, pointing to the frying pan as he went by. Tom wasn't listening to her.

"I'll just be a minute. I just want to make a drink. It'll be my last one before dinner," he slurred while Emma took a step back, away from him.

"Father, you can't keep doing this. You can't keep coming home here every night after your trip to the office to have lunch with your cronies, and get a couple of drinks there and then a few more after work, and a couple on the train, and one for the road at wherever it is you go when you get off the train. It's too much. It's just too much on me, and it's really too much on you—that is, unless you are simply trying to kill yourself. I'm frightened, Father, I really am," she pleaded, nearly at the point of tears.

Tom found what he was looking for. He opened the bottle and poured himself a scotch. He went into the freezer and got out the ice and tossed a cube into his drink and walked out to the dining room table and sat down. Emma was beside herself. She followed him into the room, ready for the confrontation.

"I'm not your wife, you know. I'll put up with only so much of this, and then I'll leave you. It's bad enough I have to make dinner every night. I'm willing to do that, but I'm not willing to sit back and watch you drink yourself into an early grave. You're an alcoholic, Father, and you need help," she told him, strongly holding her ground as she stood over him.

Tom took a drink and put the glass down. He turned his face and looked up into her eyes. "Don't you have any idea at all how difficult this has been for me? Can't you even begin to imagine what it's like for me?" he petitioned.

Emma was somewhat moved by his plea. She sat down in the chair next to him and reached over and took hold of his glass. "Father, if you don't think I have any feeling for you, any sense of what you're going through, then you must be crazy. Of course I do, but that's not the point here. This is the point, what I'm holding here in my hand, that's the point, Father. The stuff inside this glass isn't going to bring her back. It's only going to destroy you, destroy us," she admonished, putting the glass down on the table.

Tom dropped his gaze down onto the glass. He sat there silent for a moment and then picked it up and took another drink. "Go in and see how dinner's coming. Go talk to your hamburgers in there," he gruffly ordered.

Emma felt a flash of anger. "You're not listening to me. You're not listening to me at all, are you?" she demanded. Tom tried to ignore her, but Emma wasn't through. "It's obvious that you're not going to do anything about it, are you?" she chided. Tom continued to go silent. Emma was becoming furious with him. "You're not going to ruin my life. You're not going to ruin my life anymore like you've always done in the past," she yelled, bolting up out of the chair. This time, she hit a nerve.

"What the hell are you talking about? What the hell are you saying, I'm not going to ruin your life anymore like I've always done in the past? That's absolute garbage, and you know it, Emma," he shouted.

Emma jumped back down into her chair and looked him straight in the eye. "Let me tell you something, Father. You've always been treating me like I was dirt, like I was always some kind of second class, second class I don't know what. This is not only about your dam drinking. Oh no, it's much deeper than that, Father, much deeper. You're drinking is a disaster. I could forgive you for that. But treating me the way you always have, putting me light-years behind Liz all this time, well, that's more than I am able to forgive. That's more than I am ever going to forgive."

"Emma, you don't know what you're talking about," Tom interrupted.

"Oh yes, I do. I've heard you on more than one occasion say to Mother what you really thought about your adopted daughter. I've heard you with my own ears say to her you only got me to appease her, that you really didn't want me but just sort of went along for the ride for her. And boy, have you ever shown it. Liz this and Liz that and Liz the lawyer and Liz the genius, and never—no, not even one time—a kind word about Emma, some recognition for Emma. No, Father, you never talked about Emma because you never cared about Emma, and Emma's getting sick of it, Emma's had enough, Emma's leaving you and this place and your whole damn life," she forcefully told him in no uncertain terms while she got up from her chair.

Tom didn't know what to say, but he knew he had to say something to try to get her back. "Emma, you're exaggerating the whole thing. You've got a pretty darn good imagination there. I told you, I'll say it again, you've got a really good imagination, and that's just what you're doing right now. You're imagining it. Oh no, not the drinking. I will admit that my drinking has gotten to be a little more over the top than it should be. Let's chalk that up to your mother's death, shall we? But on count two, the 'I don't care about Emma' charge, and on count three, 'I never wanted Emma in the first place,' well, you see, Emma, there is just no evidence to support those charges. I plead innocent to both counts," he said, trying to somewhat make light of the situation to win her back.

Emma wasn't buying it. "Father, you can't sweet-talk your way out of reality. Words and deeds, they have consequences, Father. They have meaning, words have feeling. I can't even begin to tell you how many times I cried myself to sleep, longing to hear one kind word from you, a little praise perhaps, on how I did this good over here or did that good over there. But it never came out from you, not even once," she lamented, trying to hold back the tears.

Tom took a sip of his drink. "Emma, I'll try to... I'll try to—"

"Try to what, Father?" she demanded.

"I'll try to...oh well, why can't you just lay off me now. My wife just died, and quite frankly, I just don't feel like continuing this conversation. Now why don't you go inside and fix dinner, and we will talk about this later," he insisted. Emma decided enough was enough. She turned from him and went back into the kitchen, over to the stove, only this time things were different. This time, he was going to pay.

"Go talk to your hamburgers in there," she mockingly said to herself, quoting what had just come out of his mouth. "We'll just see how much he likes it when he has to get Liz in here. I'll be out of here by tomorrow," she vowed, placing the food on a plate and bringing it in to him before she went upstairs.

A few days had passed, and the campus at Central seemed almost deserted considering the time of the year. The cold north wind swept across relentlessly, causing even the hardiest of students to head for shelter. The cold weather resembled early January, and the headline of the day was the scientific community's warning about the possibility of another ice age. Things certainly appeared bleak that morning as Emma got off the bus and walked across Kingsley Boulevard with her classmate.

"Looks like we're going to have an early winter this year. I hate winter, don't you, Emma?" Kate complained.

Kate Brown was an outgoing, very bright, very good-looking young woman with an independent streak a mile wide. "You said it," Emma replied, feeling a shiver from the cold go up her back.

Kate started to walk faster in spite of the fact that they both struggled with the wind. "I almost didn't come in today with the damn weather. I guess I just can't get enough of Mrs. Saunders' calculus class. That must really be it," she joked.

Emma had just about had it with the conditions. "I would have stayed home today myself, except for the fact that I can't take living with my father. Ever since my mother died, he has been impossible," she struggled to tell her, nearly gasping for air in the cold.

"Come on, Emma, let's get inside. Let's get inside Bowman Hall. We're early. We can sit and talk, and maybe a coffee or two wouldn't be a bad idea either," Kate suggested.

Emma nodded at her, and they made their way up the hill as quickly as they could. They passed through the door and walked a short distance and entered the student lounge. "I'll get the coffee, yours is…"

"Light milk, no sugar."

"Good, then you get the table, and I'll be with you in a minute," Kate said.

Emma headed over to a quiet table toward the rear and waited for Kate to return. She sat there thinking about how bad her father had become. She told herself it wasn't her fault, but somehow, she still felt a pang of guilt, and she just couldn't understand where it was coming from. She looked across the room and saw that Kate would be a little longer. No, her father was definitely not her fault, she told herself, trying to strengthen her resolve for whatever eventuality was going to take place. Then her mind shifted to her birth mother, and she thought to herself that if only she could find her, if only they could connect, somehow this terrible nightmare would turn into a happy ending.

A moment or two went by, and Kate returned to her at the table. "This should help," her friend said, placing the two cups of coffee on the table.

Emma forced a smile and took a drink. "That's hot, but it's pretty good too. Thanks for the coffee, Kate. My turn next time," she said.

Kate sat down and stared into her eyes. "So what were you saying out there on the tundra about living with your father? What's going on with that one?" Kate asked her sympathetically. Emma took another sip and thought to herself, why not go into it? What difference would it make?

"He's hit rock bottom with my mother gone. He used to drink more than he should, but now, forget it. He's an alcoholic who just doesn't give a damn and he's very demanding and he's on this insane pilgrimage to the altar of my older sister, Elizabeth. He goes around making sure everybody knows just how great she is, when in fact, she's a complete waste," Emma announced in a most deprecating way.

Kate felt sorry for her. She had come to like her ever since they had gotten to know each other on the bus. "Do you want to hear what I would do if I were you?" Kate asked. Emma nodded her approval. "I would confront him to clean up his act."

"Been there, done that," Emma interrupted. Kate was surprised.

"It must be worse than I first thought. Well then, Emma, if that didn't or doesn't work, I mean you can always try again."

"That won't work. Trying again will just lead to another fight with zero positive results," Emma told her, interrupting a second time. Kate leaned back in her chair and exhaled a deep breath.

"Then you've really only got one alternative, Emma. If I were you and all else failed, like you're telling me, then what you need to do is move out. Flat-out move out, and that's all there is to it. The man must be an idiot to throw you away, but apparently that's exactly what he's doing," Kate said, trying to reassure her.

Emma couldn't find any fault with her logic. "That's what I've been telling myself, Kate. On the other hand, if I move out, I'll have to pay rent. That means a job. It also could mean bye-bye to college. I've always had good grades. I know I can maintain them, but I do need to open a book once in a while, especially for things like Mrs. Saunders' world. I don't know if I could handle everything all at once," Emma said, sounding like someone pretty well consumed with their own self-doubt.

Kate was very understanding. "I see what you mean. I see what you've got going here. It's not too good, that's for sure, Emma, but there is hope, so don't give up. However, you do need to remember one thing. You can't let him make a slave out of you. You're not his wife, you're his daughter."

"Adopted daughter," Emma injected. Kate was unrattled by that.

"Still, his daughter and he has to be made well aware of that fact and those boundaries, and if after that the shit hits the fan, then you have no choice but to get the hell out," she admonished.

95

Emma nodded her head in resignation as she looked down at her watch. "Thanks again, Kate. Thanks for listening. You're really a good friend. I'll get through it somehow, don't worry. I promise I will. Now I don't want to keep my good friend from her calculus class, the one that she loves so much, so we'd better get going," Emma told her, and the two young women got up to start their day.

It was heading toward late afternoon that same day. Liz was sitting at her desk in the apartment working on her social calendar in between glances at the large textbook on the desk. The late afternoon light entering the room from the one small window gave off a muted glow, creating an austere feeling, a feeling conducive to study. Liz seemed content in this atmosphere, having the apartment all to herself, in one of those rare moments. She jotted a note into her day planner and returned to her textbook. She wanted to concentrate on the case work before her, but her imagination kept slipping off in a different direction. She told herself to be strong, to prioritize, to put him into the back of her mind, but it wasn't so easy. Try as she might, her thoughts kept returning to Steve, along with a burning vision of him handing a piece of paper to Emma when she had left him unguarded at the Red Fox restaurant, where her mother's family gathering had taken place a few days before.

The thoughts of betrayal eventually began to subside, and Liz replaced them with a new game she invented for herself, a game that took the form of diary entries in her planner for the best way to destroy them both if Steve ever left her for her sister. A certain type of serene state came over her now that she was more convinced that the unthinkable could never fully materialize. Liz returned to a more calm, peaceful state, and the room became a quiet, welcome friend again, along with her law book.

"Liz, let me in," Sally Winters' voice boomed out from behind the front door. "I'm stuck out here, I left my key," she yelled out, pounding on the door with her fist.

Liz looked up from her book and shook her head. "Damn it," she cried out to herself at the interruption. She got up and went to the front door. "Sally, what are you doing out there?" she mockingly asked her as she pulled on the lock and opened the door.

Sally was relieved that her roommate was there. "Thank goodness you're home, Liz. I was changing bags, you know me, always the organized one, and, well, you can figure out the rest of the story," she said, walking to her side of the apartment, taking off her coat. Liz hurried over to her desk and closed her day planner.

"So, Liz, is the big date still on? Is Steve coming at five for your romantic interlude?" Sally sarcastically asked her.

Liz was in no mood for her antics. "You know, Winters, you're beginning to annoy me. No, you're really beginning to annoy me. In fact, instead of calling you Sally, I think I might start calling you Joan, as in that little bitch Joan McCarthy," Liz chastised her.

Sally's face changed to feigned sadness, but inside, she reveled in the attention. "Something's eating you, Liz. What's wrong, Steve called and canceled?" she provoked.

Liz began to laugh at her. "You only wish you had a guy like Steve, or anything else resembling a guy, for that matter. You know, come to think of it, I've never once seen you with a guy. And you know, I can't even remember you ever even talking about one unless you're flapping your trap about my boyfriend. What are you, some kind of a lesbian or something? You and that dipshit McCarthy would be my guess," Liz challenged her.

Sally ignored her. "Seems like we're getting a little testy today, Miss Elizabeth. Could be it's not about le beau Steve at all. Could be you're having trouble mastering that enormous textbook lying over there on your desk. Why, I do declare that could be even more catastrophic than losing a boyfriend, even a good-looking one for that matter," Sally bantered in her most polished Southern accent.

Liz started to laugh. "You'd never make it in Gone with the Wind or any other movie role that I can think of, Winters. You're just too much of an intellectual wannabe for that," Liz shot back at her.

Sally was in her element with her. "Okay, Molloy, let's stop screwing around here. What's the scoop? What's the story with Steve? Is he coming, going? Are you in, are you out? Tell me as your closest friend and confidant, and I promise to never tell Joan McCarthy a single word. I promise, and that's a promise I will instantly fail to keep the minute I pry it out of you," Sally said, laughing to herself.

Liz sat at her desk and looked down into her book. "I don't care what you tell that idiot McCarthy, but you may as well know that I'm in because he's going to be here in a few minutes, and we're going over to Franks for an early dinner together," Liz boasted, looking down at her watch.

Sally was impressed. "So Mr. Wonderful is coming here. This is my first chance to look him over for you, since you obviously don't have very much natural talent at things, and you obviously need my opinion on anything of this nature. I'll check him out for you, free of charge—that is, at least until I think of something worth getting in return." Sally pushed her.

Liz looked over at her with a superior smirk. "I seriously doubt I'll ever need your opinion on men," she announced, feeling really good inside with that one.

Sally went right along. "Maybe yes, maybe no," she replied just as the front doorbell rang. Sally closed her textbook and put it and her planner into the drawer. "Well, aren't you going to get it?" Sally nervously asked her as Liz locked her desk drawer and got up.

"Just keep your big mouth shut while he's here, or I'll kill you," Liz scolded, walking over to the door. She took hold of the handle and took a deep breath and then opened the door.

"Hi, Liz, I'm a tad early but I got through my class a little quicker than expected. Hope that's okay," Steve said, stepping inside the apartment.

Liz smiled at him. "We're good. I just was finishing up myself," she said, letting him in and walking over to her roommate. "Steve, this is Sally. Sally, this is Steve. Sally and I have been roommates for, well, since I first came here to Columbia. Sally is prelaw also. She's almost as good a student as me," Liz said, in her most polite introductory form.

"Nice to meet you, Steve. Liz has told me a little about you. Hope to see you around," Sally said, purposefully keeping it short. Liz was relieved.

"Well, now that we've all gotten to know one another, what do you say we get going, Steve? I don't want to make it too late. It's only Monday, and we have a long week ahead of us," Liz said, pushing Steve out the door. Then she stepped back inside and looked over at the young woman. "See you later, Sally, and don't wait up—that is, just in case we decide to run off to Rome tonight," Liz quipped, setting her roommate straight in her mind.

"She seems all right," Steve innocently said as they began walking to the restaurant. Liz took it in stride.

"You're right, she's almost the perfect type of person for me to have to share the room with. She's very bright and she likes to battle, keeps me on my toes," Liz admitted.

Steve laughed. "She'll probably make a good lawyer then, I mean, the 'liking to battle' part," he said.

Liz saw an opportunity to put Sally in check. "Yeah, you're probably right with that one, but the other thing that makes her a good roommate to have is that she's a lesbian. Not too blatant but, nevertheless, a full-fledged, dyed-in-the-wool lesbian. She doesn't date, so that's good for me, no boys over, and she doesn't have any of the other over either, which is also good. I wouldn't stand for that. We got this all agreed to on day one, and so far, so good. So for me, it's peace and quiet and plenty of time to study if I'm ever going to get my jurisprudence and jurisprudence my way into taking over for Father," she told him.

Steve laughed as he threw his arm around her shoulder. They took a few steps farther, and then Steve took his arm away. "Come on, it's getting cold, let's pick up the pace a bit," he coaxed her. Liz was a bit dismayed, but she followed along.

"Okay, Speedy Gonzales, we're going to get there. Take it easy, will you?" Liz blurted, coming to a stop. Steve stopped and stood beside her.

"Okay, Liz, you win. Now what's that look on your face? You look like you want to tell me something."

"Ask you something," she said.

Steve smiled at her. "Sounds important. Okay then, ask me something. So, my charming dear lady, what is it you want to ask me?" he playfully questioned.

Liz took a somewhat nervous, deep breath. "I wanted you to take me someplace special to me on this coming Saturday, silly, that's all. I want you to take me to the Met, the Metropolitan Museum. I want to see an exhibit there. This weekend is it. Sunday is the last day, and I've been dying to see it. It's on the French impressionists. It would really mean a lot to me," she persuaded.

Steve's face dropped. He wasn't ready for this one, nor was he a big museum fan. "I'm not quite sure what I'll be doing this weekend," he weakly came back with. "I'm supposed to be going out with my brother, I think, on Saturday. I'll have to check, but I think I told him Saturday, and Sunday is out of the question. I told my parents I'd have dinner with them in Malba, at the house, so you see—"

"Yes, I think I see. Well, it was just a thought," Liz said, covering up.

Steve grabbed her shoulder and pulled her closer to him. "It's okay, Liz. It's only one weekend. There will be others. Come on, let's get over to Frank's joint. I'm starving," he said, trying to deflect the fallout.

Liz looked up at him and then pulled back and turned away. She started walking briskly toward the restaurant, wondering just what she really meant to him. "Come on, slowpoke," she blandly called out to him, never looking back to see if he was following.

"Liz, wait up," Steve called out to her. Liz slowed her pace a little but kept on walking. Steve began to run after her. "Where do you think you're going? I thought we had a dinner date," he said, getting in front of her.

Liz was happy he had chased after her, but she certainly wasn't about to show it. "We—"

"We're still on?" Steve questioned her.

Liz felt more confident. She allowed herself a small smile. "Yes, of course, we're still on, you idiot," she told him, hoping to really gain control.

Emma was sitting in the empty house alone on the living room sofa. She had returned home from school that same afternoon, feeling more determined than ever to take her fate into her own hands. She kept thinking back to her morning in the student lounge with Kate Brown and recalled Kate telling her that if it were Kate's call to make, Kate would leave home, no questions asked. It not only made sense to her, but it also bolstered Emma's confidence. After all, Emma reasoned, wasn't Kate just reiterating what she herself already knew, what she herself had already decided on? No, Emma thought, it was too late, the die was cast. She got up from the sofa and looked around the room, trying to remember better days in the past, days when Pat was there for her in so many ways that she was only now beginning to understand. It saddened her even more, but she knew she couldn't go back, she couldn't stay, that he would never change.

Emma went to the hall closet and put on her coat and then left the house. She walked up to Forest View Turnpike and then a few blocks to the east, passing the car dealership, the bank, and the apartment building until she got to Marino's Diner, and then she walked in and went up to the register.

"I saw your sign for the waitress job in the window. Who can I talk to about it?" she politely asked the woman behind the counter.

The fifty-something-year-old lady smiled at her. "You don't look like no waitress," she stated, eyeing Emma up and down.

"I'm a good worker," Emma countermanded in the calmest composure she could muster.

The woman nodded at her. "That's good. You've certainly got the looks for it," she said while taking a check from one of her customers and making the change. "All right, um, say, what's your name, miss?" she asked Emma in her broken English. Emma smiled politely and told her. The woman nodded. "Emma. I like that," she said, stepping out from behind the counter and gently taking hold of her arm. "Come on with me, Emma, and you'll get to meet Joe. He's the owner. My name is Matilda, and what I say goes around here, and Joe knows it. So if I want to get you hired, I get you hired, and if I don't want to get you hired, you don't get hired," she boasted.

Emma laughed a nervous little laugh to humor her. "So, Matilda, what say you about me? Do you want to get me hired?" she inquisitively asked, playing right along.

The matronly woman stopped in the aisle between two tables and turned toward her and looked up. "Oh, honey, don't worry about a thing. You're in. Trust me. When Joe sees you, you'd even be in without me having to twist his arm," she extolled.

About an hour went by before Tom Molloy returned home. "Emma, I'm here," he shouted, removing his coat in front of the closet. "Emma," he called out again, only to receive more of the same silence as before. He hung his coat and walked around into the kitchen, expecting to see her there. Funny, he thought to himself, taking out an unopened bottle of scotch and reaching for a glass. Tom finished making his drink and meandered out into the living room and sat down in his favorite chair.

Where the hell could that girl be? he asked himself, taking a drink. He put the glass down and got up and went back into the kitchen. He looked down at the answering machine and saw there were no messages, so he went back to his chair. The drink could use a little more ice, he thought, but he didn't feel like getting up again, so he sat and pondered about Emma. The still house began to rankle his nerves. It seemed too quiet, too empty. He looked around and tried to picture his wife, hoping that somehow, someway she could make contact with him, even appear to him, but he knew that was impossible, and so he tried to concentrate on the big case he was overseeing at the office. But even that didn't work, and his mind seemed to control itself and keep on course, right back to his daughter, Emma.

He looked at his watch and saw that it was almost six. She must be coming home soon; no message, no note. It won't be much longer, he tried to convince himself, but all the while, an uneasy feeling was gaining the upper hand, and all the what-if questions flooded his mind. Tom began to realize that he felt frightened—no, even terrorized at the prospect of being all alone in the house with nobody else there, only himself, Tom Molloy. The silence was deafening, almost too much to bear. Suddenly, the phone rang out loud. Tom's heart raced as he leaped up from the chair and ran into the kitchen, desperately hoping to hear his daughter's voice. He picked up the phone and answered.

"Hello," he anxiously blurted into the handpiece.

"Is Louis there?" a Spanish-sounding man asked, barely discernible to him.

Tom got angry. "There's no Louis here. Why don't you know who you're dialing? You've got the wrong number, you moron," Tom shouted, slamming down the phone. He went over to the other counter and grabbed the bottle of scotch and took it into the living room. He sat back down in his chair and put the bottle on the end table. Then he looked up at the ceiling and took a deep breath.

"Dear God, where is she? Bring her back to me. Bring Emma back," he pleaded.

A few more minutes went by, and Tom could hear keys jingling in the latch. He turned his head and could see the lock move. He jumped up and ran to the door and opened it. "Emma, is everything all right?" he exclaimed.

Emma was surprised with his demeanor. She entered and walked past him into the living room and took off her coat. "Things are just fine, Father. How was your day?" she casually remarked, feeling a bit guilty over the deeds she had just done.

Tom followed her into the room and sat down and sipped his drink. Emma carried her coat over and hung it in the closet and then reentered the room. "Okay, young lady, let's have it. Out with it. I come home, and you're missing. No note, no call, what gives, Emma?" he demanded.

Emma sat on the sofa, not really sure how to handle it. "Oh, things are fine. School is fine. I'm fine. I suppose you're fine too," she blurted, trying her best to keep her composure while deciding just how much to tell him.

"Don't be so funny, Emma. Now what are you going to do about dinner?" he questioned, taking another drink.

Emma felt like she had to get away and retreat into the kitchen. She got up and looked at him, feeling like he was almost a pathetic figure. "I'm going to make chicken tonight. Chicken and rice and peas. You like peas. I think I'll cook peas tonight. Besides, they're easy, and I want to do some studying later," she said, turning away from him and heading toward the kitchen.

"You still haven't told me where you've been," her father called out. Emma froze in her tracks. "But then again, I suppose you're a big girl now, and I don't need to know your every whereabout. Chicken will be fine. Only get a move on it, I'm starved," he insisted.

Emma was tremendously relieved at catching the break. She started quickly walking toward the kitchen again. Tom took a drink and leaned back in his chair. "I got a call today from Liz at the office. Things are going really well for her. She may stop by here at the house in a week or two. It'll be great seeing her, don't you think, Emma?" he called out to her.

Emma stopped again in her tracks. She took in a deep breath and held it a few seconds before exhaling. She pictured in her mind the small apartment in that quaint two-family house she had just rented from a lovely older couple after leaving the diner. Then she let her breath out and turned back around toward her father.

"Yeah, Father, sounds great. It will certainly be great to see her, really great to see her. I can hardly wait," she fabricated and then she walked into the kitchen, determined more than ever to carry out her plan.

Tom reached over and picked up a magazine from the end table and tried to read it, but his mind just wandered. He closed his eyes and pictured his wife, Pat, but her image soon faded, and he restlessly returned to the magazine and the article on aging gracefully. Once again, his mind wandered. He began to think about the exchange he had just had with Emma. She certainly didn't seem very happy hearing that Liz would be coming for a visit, he thought to himself. If only Emma had followed Liz into law, things would be different; they would be better. The two of them would be close, and he would have a second assistant with him, he told himself.

Too bad, but at least Emma was here and able to take care of the house, the cooking, the cleaning, and the rest of it, he surmised. At least she was still here to do the work, he chuckled to himself. No, maybe better the two of them went their separate ways. It might have made things even more difficult if they were together, he decided, taking a drink and finishing his glass. He put the magazine back on the table and went into the kitchen to pour a refill.

"I thought you said we were getting chicken tonight, Emma. That looks like hamburger to me," he complained while making another drink. Emma felt a little flustered.

"I didn't defrost any today. I didn't get around to it," she defended.

"How long till we eat?"

"Shortly, Father, we'll be eating shortly. Why don't you just go inside and sit down, and dinner will be in just a few minutes. Can you do that? Can you just go in and sit down, please?" Emma impatiently responded.

Tom didn't take the hint. "What is it with you, Emma. Are you like this because your sister wants to come home and pay us a visit, or are you just plain miserable, a cranky, miserable little pain in the ass? What is it with you, anyway, Emma?" he demanded.

Emma had just about had it with him. "Do you want to know why it's hamburger and not chicken? Okay then, I'll tell you why. It's hamburger because nothing else could get defrosted by me as usual, and that's because I was signing a rental agreement on an apartment near the diner, where it just so happens I landed a job. And just for your information, Father, the people who own the home, the two-family, the landlords, that is, well, they are very nice people, an older couple, and they said I can come over anytime I want to and start living there even before the beginning of the month. So guess what, I'm out of here first thing in the morning. Thank you, and I do mean thank you, because now I won't have to put up with you and Liz—or is it Liz and you? You'll have to check back later for the answer to that one, Father," she sarcastically announced, walking past him and putting only one plate out on the dining room table.

Tom was furious. "You mean to tell me that after all I've done for you, you're just going to up and leave? You're just going to quit school and throw your life away being a dishwasher—"

"A waitress," she interrupted.

"Okay then, a waitress. What the hell difference does it make? After all your mother and I have done for you, now this. The next thing you know, you'll be out on the street. You aren't going to be any waitress for long, that's for sure. In fact, you're not going to be a waitress at all, not even for five minutes. And the apartment, forget it. You're not getting any apartment. And if I have even one ounce of trouble from those bastards who rented it to you, I'll take them apart legally, and they'll be the ones who'll be out on the street. Do you understand me?" he threatened.

Emma came back into the kitchen and filled up her plate. "Well, now that the cat's out of the bag, I actually feel better. It's wonderful. Who could have imagined it?" she gleefully teased, while Tom's blood continued to boil.

"Emma, you stupid little girl, do you have any idea just how vulnerable you would be out there on your own, working in that crummy diner? I've got news for you, you little idiot, I've been in that diner over there on the turnpike, and it's got some pretty unsavory characters in it. Why, you must be out of your mind. No, it's out of the question, you're not leaving home, you're not quitting school, and you're not going to work at that sleazy diner or anything even remotely resembling that sleazy diner, and I'm going to make dam sure of that no matter what it takes. So get used to it, Emma, and cut the crap," he blasted, walking out into the dining room.

Emma picked up her plate and took it up to her room. Tom sat alone at his table, taking deep breaths, trying to get his blood pressure down. He leaned forward with both elbows on the table and cupped his hands over his face. She wasn't going to really do it, he tried to tell himself, and besides, if she did, he would stop her, he reiterated over and over. No, there was no way on earth he would let her leave. And besides, she was a reasonable girl, she did well in school, she was interested in writing, she liked her teachers. No, she wouldn't possibly do anything this foolish. She was probably making the whole thing up in that vivid little imagination of hers, he thought, taking his first bite. If only Pat were still alive, Pat could handle her better, he lamented.

He took a drink and pictured Liz in his mind. Better if Liz were home, anyway. She was always easier to deal with, he rationalized to himself. Maybe Liz would want to come home if she knew that this one was out of here, he thought. But no, that was probably out of the question. No, Tom concluded, he was stuck with Emma, so he had better try and make the best of it. He took another drink and got up from the table. He climbed the stairs and made his way down the hall to Emma's room. The door was closed, so he knocked. Emma didn't answer. Tom knocked a second time.

"Emma, it's me, your father. Can I come in?" he asked her.

"All right, but don't try talking me into anything. My mind's made up, Father," she answered.

Tom took a deep breath. "Pat, if you can hear me, do something and do it quickly," he anxiously whispered to himself, and then he entered the room. "Emma, not for my sake but for yours, won't you reconsider? Please. Please reconsider, Emma. We can make things a lot better around here. Don't go throwing your life away just to prove a point. What about school? What about that? How are you going to succeed in anything by burning the candle at both ends? You know, they say that youth is wasted on the young. And you know, in most cases, that's true. Don't let it be true for you, Emma. You're too good for that. We can cancel any arrangements you may have made. They can't come back to bite us. I'm sure of that. So please, Emma, don't do this to yourself. Don't cut off your nose to spite your face. It isn't worth it," he quietly told her, and then he turned and left the room.

The next morning saw a beautiful sunrise over Flushing, with exquisite shades of pink filling the sky, painting in the spaces between the fluffy white clouds. The bus stopped at the corner, and the two young women got off together.

"So, Kate, did I do the right thing?" Emma asked her.

Kate grabbed her arm and jerked her forward, crossing against the light. "Come, Emma, let's move it," she shouted, and they ran across the boulevard to the campus side of the street. "What did you say?" Kate asked, gasping for breath.

"Did I do the right thing?"

"You moved out, right?" Kate asked.

Emma started walking. "No, not exactly, but I told him I was going to, that I got an apartment and a job."

"How'd that go over," Kate questioned, walking alongside her friend.

Emma looked up at the sky and saw how beautiful it was. "It went over like a lead balloon. He freaked out. Then he started barking more orders about me never leaving, and then he gave me the encyclopedia version of all he and my mother had done for me and how could I do this—"

"Et cetera, et cetera," Kate interrupted.

Emma nodded. "You've got the picture. It was a complete disaster," Emma told her.

Kate grabbed her arm again and stopped walking. "What did you expect? He's only looking out for himself. You have to do what you think is best for you. And if you ask me, what's best for you is to go through with it. You've gone this far for a reason, and the reason is definitely not because things are so great at home," Kate lectured.

Emma looked back up at the pink sky. "You're right, Kate. You're right. He almost tripped on the rug during the last round when he came up to my room to make his final plea. Between his neediness and his drinking."

Kate's ears went up. "You say drinking? Forget it. You can't stay there alone if he's got a drinking problem. My aunt has one. She's impossible. You can't go near her even when she just looks at a bottle. It's a disease with really bad consequences. If I were you, I'd get my ass moving forward, and I wouldn't look back. I see you've been looking up at the sky. It's beautiful this morning, isn't it? I mean, the pinks, the whites, and the blue. Take it as an omen, Emma, a good omen. Take it to mean that the positive energy you are looking up at will guide you to a better life, and everything else will just fall into place," Kate advised, hugging her for the very first time before she turned and resumed walking to class.

The same pink sky showed up that morning in the big borough, the one that was home to Columbia. Liz squirmed as she sat in the history class, pretending to listen to the lecture about the economic reasons for the French Revolution. She impatiently looked down at her watch and counted the minutes until the dreadful exercise would end. A handsome young man a few seats away turned his head toward her and smiled. Liz instantly looked away, returning to what was really on her mind, the two people she had to deal with—Steve, her fickle boyfriend, and Emma, her insubordinate sister making a play for him.

Liz closed her notebook and tapped her feet on the floor, impatiently waiting for the session to end. Maybe Steve really did have plans with his family, she reasoned, but then again, why wasn't she included in those plans? He didn't seem so interested until she walked away, she remembered. It was only then that he came after her last night, she counseled in her mind. No, something wasn't quite right, she thought, and that something might very possibly have the name Emma written all over it.

"Liz, we can go now, lecture's over. Hello," the young woman sitting next to her said.

Liz was embarrassed. "I must have been daydreaming, Jenny. Thanks. I'm all right, I'll see you back here Thursday. Thanks again," Liz reiterated, rising to her feet to escape to the outside. She quickly made her way through the corridor and went out the main door. She began walking diagonally over toward another one of the stoic buildings on the historic site to get to her next class.

"Liz, I thought I saw you," Sally Winters called out to her.

Liz turned and waved as Sally approached her with Joan McCarthy. Liz gathered herself and felt like she was ready for them. "Hi, Sally, Joan. What's up with you guys?" Liz asked.

Sally went right for it. "I didn't get to talk to you last night. I ended up going out myself, got back late, and hit the hay. You were out cold, sleeping like a baby, and you left so early this morning that I missed you a second time. So tell me, how'd it go last night? He's awfully good-looking—for a guy, I mean," Sally prodded.

Liz wouldn't allow herself to become flustered. She looked her in the eye and smiled. "Great, it went really great. What'd you expect? He took me to dinner. I know what you're thinking, he took me to Frank's, big deal, but you know what, it went really well. That boy is captivated, yeah, that's the right word. He's captivated, he even picked up the check," Liz bragged.

McCarthy chuckled. "Sounds like he's hot to trot or maybe too hot to handle," she exclaimed, breaking into a louder laugh.

Sally joined in with her. "Sounds like you did all right, sister. Well, thanks for the breaking news, but we've got to get moving. I'll catch you later back at the barn, you little heartbreaker, you," Sally teased, walking away from her with McCarthy, who then turned back while she was still laughing. "Don't do anything I wouldn't do, Liz. It might get you into some hot water, real hot water," she called out as Liz made her hasty retreat away from them.

X

It was early that afternoon when Emma returned home from Central. She put the key in the door, turned the lock, and rushed in. She ran up the stairs and pulled out a suitcase that she had hidden under the bed. She opened her dresser and took out the clothes in the second drawer and placed them inside the suitcase. Then she did the same thing for the first drawer, where she collected her jewelry, scarf, gloves, and other small items. When the suitcase was filled, she placed it back under the bed, carefully hiding it. She looked at her watch and then ran down the stairs and out the front door, barely remembering to lock it.

She made her way down the street to Forest View Turnpike and headed for the diner with a planned pit stop at the O'Leary's, her new landlords-to-be, whose rental sign she had spotted on her way to her job interview at Marino's. She turned up the side street and, in an instant, walked up onto the porch and rang the bell of the red brick, two-family house. A short, older woman with white hair pulled the door open.

"Emma, so nice to see you. We were wondering—"

"Wondering if I was going to go through with it? Well, Mrs. O'Leary, I guess so because I'm here," Emma interrupted.

The older woman smiled at her. "I'll call Jack. He'll be happy to see you, dear," the motherly figure said.

Emma was too rushed for time. "Thank you, Mrs. O'Leary, thank you, but that won't be necessary. I'm in a hurry to get to my new job. I just wanted to stop by and tell you that I'll be coming in—moving in, I should say— tonight, about dinnertime or a little after, if that's okay with you," Emma stated.

The woman seemed happy. "Yes, that's fine, dear. Only one thing. Leave the Mrs. O'Leary stuff at the front door and call me Rose from now on. It would be more to my liking," she said in her mild Irish brogue.

Emma was relieved. "Thanks again, and I'll see you later," she replied, quickly turning to leave.

The older woman had already developed a fondness for her. "Wait, Emma, before you go running off, just one other thing," she said.

Emma immediately stopped and turned back around toward her. "Yes, Mrs. O'Leary—I mean, Rose," Emma said.

Rose nodded her head at her. "And don't forget what we talked about when you first came by. You stay here as long as you like, as long as you feel you need to. If things change— and I hope for your sake they do change for the better—then you can leave at any time. You can leave to go home to your father, or you can leave for any other reason. But Jack and I talked it over, and we won't be holding you to the rental paper should you ever need to make a move. We were both young once, too, you know," the kindly woman told her.

Emma felt herself well up inside. She could feel the onset of tears begin to fill her eyes, tears she desperately fought to hold back. "Thank you again, thank you so much," Emma sincerely told her, and then she turned and quickly walked out to the sidewalk to get over to the diner.

The traffic whizzed by on Forest View Turnpike as Emma ran toward her new job. She entered through the front door and went over to the register to a waiting Matilda, who happened to be fighting with a customer over the check.

"What do you mean you didn't have soup?" Matilda blasted the middle-aged man. "Jenny, you wrote the check, the man had soup, right? Just like it says so here. Mister, what do you think this is, a charity? We're running a business here. Now give me two fifty, or I'll call the cops," Matilda screamed at him.

The man turned beet red. He reached into his pocket and pulled out three dollars and slammed it on the counter in front of her. "Here, you fat bitch, keep the change. This is for your retirement fund at the old fat lady's home," he retaliated before storming out.

Matilda wasn't flustered one bit. She picked up the money and put it into the register. "Jenny, I'd like you to meet Emma. Emma is going to start working here today. Put her in section four, next to you, and keep an eye on her—help her out, I mean. I think you two should get along nicely. And don't forget, Jenny, any questions, come and get me. Don't go to Joe," she instructed, pulling out an official diner shirt and handing it to Emma.

Jenny was a friendly-looking young woman, about Emma's age. "Nice to meet you, Emma. Come on, follow me. You can change in the back," she said, and the two women headed to what passed for a dressing room. Jenny opened the door to the small room and walked in and turned on the light. "So how'd you happen to come here—I mean, get the waitress job here? They've been trying to fill it for a month. No takers. And then lo and behold, they've got you," she told Emma while snapping the chewing gum inside her mouth.

Emma tried to smile at her. "How are the tips? How much—no, let me rephrase that. Are you full-time or part-time?" Emma asked her.

"Full-time," she answered. Emma started to change into her new diner shirt.

"How much a week do you make?" Emma asked.

Jenny's face lit up with a smile. "I do pretty good here. I'd say on the average week, I'm making about two hundred, sometimes two fifty, say, like at the holidays or something like that," Jenny told her.

Emma finished with the shirt change. "And tell me, Jenny, before we go out there, what's it like, or, I mean, how bad is it working for Matilda?" Emma nervously inquired.

Jenny laughed and put her hand on Emma's shoulder. "It's not Matilda you've got to worry about around here. Her bark is worse than her bite. No, Matilda is a pussycat compared to that bastard Joe," Jenny confided.

Emma took a step back; her face suddenly changed to a look of consternation. "Joe, the boss, I mean, the owner?"

"Yeah, that Joe. Joe the owner. He thinks he owns you, the little greaseball," Jenny told her.

"What do you mean, Jenny? You can tell me, I swear I won't say a word," Emma instinctively pushed her.

Jenny hesitated a minute and then looked her in the eye. "Come on, we've got to go, but I'm going to trust you. I remember what it was like when I started working here. I didn't know the ropes either. Anyway—and trust me, I never said this—Joe thinks he's a big ladies' man, you know, like we're all just dying to sleep with him—"

"That little gargoyle," Emma interrupted.

"What's a gargoyle?" Jenny asked her, looking somewhat perplexed.

Emma just shook her head. "It's an ugly, little creature right out of the Middle Ages. Anyhow, that's beside the point. So tell me, Jenny, what's the scoop on Joe?" Emma questioned.

The young waitress had a serious look on her face. "I'll tell you this about Joe. If he ever grabs your ass and you complain about it, out you go. Oh, it doesn't happen very often, but every now and then, old Joe gets a little too friendly for a nice girl's taste, if you know what I mean," Jenny warned her, and then she turned and opened the door to walk out of the room, leaving Emma there wondering about just what she had gotten herself into.

Liz pulled out her key and unlocked her apartment door. She walked in and saw that Sally was already there sitting at her desk. "First time we've actually crossed paths on campus," Sally said to her as she took off her coat and placed her book on her desk.

"First time for everything, only why did it have to be with Joan McCarthy? That girl gives me the creeps—"

"I like her," Sally interrupted, getting up from her chair and walking over to Liz's side of the room. "So let's really have it with that boyfriend of yours. I know you pretty well, Liz. Did it really go well, or was that just the edited version with McCarthy standing there in your face?" Sally queried.

Liz didn't want to go into it at first, but then she changed her mind. "Oh, what the hell. What difference does it make? It didn't go so well, but keep it quiet, promise," Liz insisted.

Sally took a somber tone. "Of course. Hey, if it gets too bad with him, you can always come over to our side," she offered.

Liz shook her head. "Thank you. I'll take that under advisement. But I really don't think so."

"Just a friendly suggestion," Sally countered.

Liz took a deep breath. "Okay, the truth is, I think he's got it for my sister. They met at the house, then they met at my mother's service, which is where I saw Steve pass a note to her. He didn't see me, which makes it worse, but anyway, I'm sure it was his phone number that he was passing. What else could it be? He was probably trying to pick her up when I was in the other room talking to my father," Liz lamented.

Sally put her hand on Liz's shoulder. "What's this sister of yours look like, anyway?" Sally asked.

Liz looked up with a sad face that told the whole story. Sally removed her hand and sat on top of her desk. "That bad, huh? She's a knockout, right?" Sally surmised.

Liz didn't hold back. "Emma, my little sister, that little adopted bundle of joy, she's got it all going for her. Knockout doesn't even begin to describe it. You know how thousands of young girls go out to Hollywood to get discovered for the movies, and practically ninety-nine percent of them come up empty? Well, Emma is in the other one percent, that's for sure," Liz divulged.

Sally felt sorry for her. "Well, you know, Liz, you could be imagining it. Steve could have been doing something else at the scene of the crime. Who knows?" Sally said, trying to comfort her as best she could.

Liz looked up at the ceiling and began to cry. Then she dropped her head down and gazed back at Sally. "You just asked, who knows, and the answer is, well, unfortunately, I do. I'm the one who knows. I can just feel it," Liz admitted.

Sally wanted to genuinely help her. "Let's go over this carefully. Did anything come up? Did you say anything that he balked at, like he was impatient with you? Did he answer anything that should have led to natural agreement with a disagreement, like he was doing you a favor? Did anything like that happen at all?" Sally interrogated.

Liz wiped the tears with her hand and thought about it. "Well, he didn't take me up on going to the Met this Saturday. I asked him to. I said I wanted to see the impressionist exhibit there."

"What did he say? How did he handle it?" Sally pushed her.

Liz pictured it clearly. "He begged off. Something about this weekend, he was supposed to see his family in Malba or something like that."

"And you said...?" Sally led her along.

Liz paused, trying to get the right words. "I told him I really wanted to see it, that this was the last weekend before it ended."

"And he...?"

"He gave me the 'I'm not a museum person' song and dance, then he went into the 'I'm going to Malba' routine. And then I walked away from him. It was out on the street before we got to the restaurant," Liz explained.

Sally's attention was piqued. "You walked away, and then what did he do? Tell me. This could be important, very important," Sally insisted. Liz got a little flustered with her and went silent. "Come on, Liz, tell me what happened next," Sally demanded, trying to jump-start her friend. Liz finally nodded at her and then got up and looked right at her.

"I walked away, about fifteen, twenty feet or so, and I heard him, and then he, like, ran up to me to catch me, and it was kiss-and-make-up time, and then we went into Frank's and ate," Liz recalled.

Sally wasn't yet finished. "Tell me about Frank's. What was he like in there? Was he nice to you? Did he change his plans for the weekend? What happened at Frank's? What did he say there, Liz?" Sally prodded her.

Liz thought to herself and laughed. "Well, he didn't tell me he wanted to get into my sister's pants, if that's what you'd like to know," Liz sarcastically said, feeling as though she had already told Sally too much.

Sally was floored by Liz's remark. "You're not the same girl I'm used to having around here," Sally blurted, sensing it was time to back off.

Liz didn't really want to hurt her. "Listen, Sally, I appreciate your listening to me and trying to help. I guess we'll never know what's what with Steve until I give it some time. I can't—rather, we can't read his mind. We can't interpret his every word. I think I'm just going to have to give it more time and see how things go, see how it all plays out," Liz told her as she told herself she wouldn't let Steve and her sister get away with it if the unthinkable ever really did begin to materialize.

It was early evening when Emma rang the doorbell at the O'Leary residence. Rose came to answer, and she let Emma in. "How'd it go, the first day on the job?" Rose cheerfully asked.

Emma looked tired, but she was happy to see a safe, supportive face in front of her. "It went okay, Rose, but I have to tell you, I'm beat. I never realized what standing on your feet all day could do to you, even at my age, but I'm sure I'll get used to it," Emma politely answered.

"Will you be staying upstairs, tonight, child," Rose asked, trying to judge her temperament, trying to see if this arrangement had a chance to work. Emma nodded at her. Rose turned and called to her husband. "Jack, Emma's here. She'll be with us starting this evening. Come in and say hello to the poor girl. She just came from her job at the diner," Rose told him as she closed the door and then motioned for Emma to come into the living room. "Make yourself at home, Emma. I don't suppose you're hungry now. They probably fed you really well over there. Jack and I have eaten there. The food isn't bad," Rose opined, keeping up her end of the small talk.

Emma sat down and leaned back on the sofa, settling into the moment's rest.

"Jack, say hello to Emma," Rose said to him. Jack was a pleasant-looking, older gentleman, who had the type of distinguished look that made you think he was your neighborhood banker.

"Glad to have you. Anything you need, just ask. I don't know if Rose told you, but we once had a daughter, a lot like you she was," he revealed in an almost melancholy voice.

Rose grabbed the old man's arm. "Oh, Jack, that was a long time ago. Don't be bothering her with that. Kelly is with the Lord now, and we'll both be joining her one of these days, if you want to know the truth," Rose announced.

Jack laughed to himself. "You're right as usual, sweetheart, but—"

"There'll be no buts about it, Mr. O'Leary. I don't want to be driving this poor child crazy while she's with us, especially not on her first night," Rose insisted to her husband, who immediately took the hint.

"Well then, I'll be leaving you two ladies and return to my basketball game on the television. Don't forget, Emma, if you need anything, just ask either one of us. Don't be afraid," he warmly told her and then he kissed his wife and left the room.

Emma was really impressed with their kindness. "I've got to tell you something, Rose," Emma said. The older woman's curiosity grabbed hold of her. She sat down next to Emma on the sofa and waited for her to come forward with what had to be some very interesting insight. Emma wanted to be as diplomatic as possible. "I'm not really sure how it's going to go over at Marino's. The girl they have training me over there, well, she tipped me off today."

"Tipped you off about what?" Rose excitedly asked her.

Emma wasn't sure if she should continue, but somehow she had a calm, trusting feeling when it came to this gentle woman. "Okay, let me tell you the whole story, at least the story that I got from the girl I already mentioned. Her name is Jenny, and she seems like a straight shooter. Jenny told me to watch out for the owner, a man named Joe. Jenny, who's about my age, she's cute and perky. Well, anyhow, Jenny let me know in no uncertain terms that Joe has a reputation for getting fresh with women, especially the women who work over there," Emma revealed.

Rose's face instantly changed to a look of someone who was shocked after suddenly hearing a bombshell. "Why, that dirty, little so and so," Rose angrily declared.

Emma could see that her new friend had her interests at heart. "It's all true. Jenny's story is all true, it has to be," Emma continued as she began to gently cry into her sleeve. Rose was beside herself at the spectacle. She put her hand on the young woman's shoulder.

"Emma, Emma dear, you said it was all true, meaning Jenny's story, it had to be."

"Yes, because..." Emma stopped, the words were too difficult.

"Because why, dear?" Rose encouraged her.

"Because it almost happened to me. The guy came on to me. It was about ten minutes before I left the place. I went over to Matilda, she's the manager or something like that over there. I told her I had to leave, that I had a few things to take care of. She told me it would be all right but to go and tell Joe, who was sitting in the back by himself. So I went back there. The place was empty. Joe looked like he had a couple of drinks in him. Anyway, he tells me to come over and sit down next to him."

"What did you tell him?" Rose interrupted.

Emma reached into her purse and pulled out a tissue and wiped away the tears. "I told him I really couldn't, that I was just informing him that I had to leave because Matilda told me to, then I told him about getting the new apartment. All of a sudden, he reached out and grabbed my arm, like he was pulling me into the booth with him. I pulled away and told him I'm not like that, and then I turned away and walked out," Emma disclosed.

Rose became extremely agitated. "That dirty, no-good, little, dirty old man," she exclaimed.

Emma didn't want her to become any more upset. "It's not that he—"

"It surely is a crime. Imagine an old man like him laying even so much as a paw on a sweet, innocent girl like you. He should be shot," Rose interrupted, feeling her blood pressure go through the roof.

Emma wanted to calm her down. She thought the best way for that was to change the subject. "I'll be all right, Rose. I think I just need a good night's sleep. I'm sorry to hear about Kelly. Jack really misses her. I can see that," Emma compassionately said.

Rose nodded at her. "If it wasn't for his faith, I don't know what he would have done, or if he'd even be here right now. Her death hit him hard, and he couldn't accept it at all, especially in the beginning. After a time, all the prayers I said for him began to pay off, and he returned to normal, but every now and again, he goes through her death, the cancer, her suffering all over again. Every now and then, he relives the whole thing. So you see, we've all got our problems, Emma. And if that Joe so much as lays a hand on you, we'll just make him wish he was never born. We'll make ourselves his problem, I can tell you that, dear," Rose said, getting up from the sofa. She patted Emma on the shoulder and walked off toward the kitchen.

In a moment, she reappeared, holding a plate filled with cold cuts and bread and the key to her apartment. "Seems like they didn't feed you after all at that dinner, did they? Here take this upstairs and enjoy it, and I'll see you in the morning," the kindly woman told her.

Emma beamed at her. "Good night, Rose, and thanks. I'll see you in the morning," Emma happily replied, getting up from the sofa. She took hold of the tray and went up the stairs to her apartment, thinking to herself how lucky she had been to find such wonderful people.

Emma unlocked the door and went in. She put the tray down on the kitchen table and took off her coat and hung it over the chair. Then she sat down and made a sandwich and bit in. She began to think about her father. She wondered how he would take her first day of so-called freedom. She got up and checked the refrigerator for something to drink. She pulled out a bottle of club soda and then reached for a glass from the cabinet. She spotted the phone lying on the counter.

"Should I or shouldn't I?" she asked herself, returning to the table. She filled her glass and looked back over to the phone and began thinking about her father again. Maybe she didn't do the right thing after all, she thought to herself. Oh sure, she could try to put off dealing with him, but somehow she knew she couldn't. It just didn't feel right. Things had gone so fast that it wasn't really her fault that she left home, but on the other hand, she was torn between that reasoning and her fear that her father might do something drastic given his predicament.

Emma took a drink and washed down the food. She got up and went to the phone, suddenly feeling a great empathy for Tom. She picked up the phone and took a deep breath, picturing her father helplessly wallowing in tears at her absence. Should she or shouldn't she? Emma asked herself. She put the phone down and turned away, but then she suddenly stopped, as if a mysterious, invisible force took over, resigning her to stop fighting it and call her father. She turned back and picked up the phone and dialed her house, almost expecting to hear the worst.

"Hello," Tom answered, sounding rather melancholy.

"Father, it's me, it's Emma," she sheepishly said.

Tom's energy level instantly shot up. "Emma, is that you? Where are you? Are you all right?" he frantically asked her.

Emma paused and took a deep breath. "Father, I'm all right. Did you read the note I left? It's going to be fine. I have an apartment a few blocks away. They are really nice people, an older couple, the O'Learys. The job is pretty good, and I took care of things at Central. I can either resume where I left off if I return within a couple of weeks or return next semester to where I left off should I choose to go back then," she told him.

Tom was beside himself, not knowing how to handle the situation. "Emma, I got your note, and I must say that a note was really not a very nice way to treat me. But okay, that's over and done with, the main thing is that you're all right, that you're safe, and that you've thought it through and—"

"I have thought through it," Emma interrupted.

Tom jumped right back in. "Then if you have thought it through, then you'll put all this nonsense aside and you'll

126

be coming home. Or have you completely lost your mind, Emma?" he ridiculed, losing his patience.

Emma's concern for him began to wane. "Aren't you at least a little proud of me that I'm out here trying to make it on my own? Didn't you once have to make a stand when you began your law business. Don't I have the same choices to make as you had when you were young? I just called to say hello and see how you were doing and to fill you in if you needed more information than was in the note. I admit, the note wasn't the greatest way to handle this, but I felt that every time I talk to you, you don't listen to me, and we just end up fighting. So, therefore, I wrote you the note. I'm sorry for not following proper protocol, but I just didn't think I could handle proper protocol, the situation, and talking it over with you. So I did it this way. Look, Father, it isn't the end of the world. I will come home to see you. I will come home and visit and hope and expect that we can become friends. I'm sorry if I hurt you, but for now, at least I'm going to try to make a go of it on my own. If you need me, call me, but please, Father, I have to work things out in my own way," she tried to explain to him.

Tom saw he couldn't move her, that she wouldn't budge, at least not now. "All right, Emma, I see that your mind is pretty well made up. I think I know the O'Learys from when I was on the parish council. Jack and Rose, I believe."

"That's them," Emma cut in.

Tom felt a little better. "All right then, Emma. But promise me one thing. One thing is all I ask. That's fair, isn't it?" Tom persuaded.

"Okay, Father, what is it?" she replied.

Tom took a brief moment to gather himself. "Promise me, Emma, that should things begin to change regarding your new outlook and you really believe you should come home and get back to normal, you'll swallow your pride and tell me you want to come home. The door will always be open for you, Emma, because I love you. Now, please, take care of yourself, and one other thing, please let me know how you're doing, and good luck," he told her in the gentlest manner he could find, and then he hung up the phone.

Emma felt her eyes well up with tears. "Take care of yourself, Father, but I have to live my own life as best I know how," she quietly said into the empty phone.

Emma slowly cleared off the kitchen table and then went into the bedroom to change into her nightgown, replaying the evening's events over and over again in her mind. She pulled down the bed and lay down, hoping to escape from all the pressures that seemed to be coming in at her from all sides. She lay awake, tossing in the bed, trying to gain some peace. She pictured in her mind a worst-case scenario with Joe at the diner. She tried fending it off by remembering Jenny and told herself that she had survived the diner without incident, and that Jenny was an attractive young woman also. So it should all work out over there after all, Emma tried convincing herself. The minutes dragged on, but still no relief came to her.

Finally, Emma got up out of the bed and went into the kitchen. She opened her handbag on the table and pulled out Steve Walsh's number and dialed it, thinking to herself that maybe things would somehow get better by finding her birth mother. The phone continued to ring, but there was no answer.

Come on, Steve, where are you? Emma called out to herself, desperately hoping for some kind of miracle to take place for her. She let it ring a few moments longer, but finally she had to hang up. She put the phone down and went back to the table and burst into uncontrollable tears. She thought to herself that there was no one anywhere for her. Oh yeah, her father had shown some signs of remorse, but she knew that would change right after she moved back. And her sister, Liz, well, that was laughable. She knew Liz only made life a competition between the two of them whenever they were together. And Steve, well, she told herself he was a nice guy, but she wasn't really attracted to him. Besides, she hated the idea of boyfriend stealing; she knew that wasn't for her.

And then she thought about school, and Kate Brown, and her writing and other classes. And it began to dawn on her that even though she had gained her independence, she had made a huge mistake; she had given up too much, paid too high a price to escape an abusive father. But what should she do now? she asked herself through the tears of desperation. She took a moment and pulled herself together. Then she cupped her hands together and looked up.

"Dear God, only You know just how far down I've come and only You can pull me back up from rock bottom. Please help me now. You're all I've got," she prayed and then she got up and went back to the phone and dialed the number again.

"Hello," the young man answered.

"Steve, is that you? It's Emma," she nervously said.

Steve was delighted to hear from her. "Emma, I was just thinking about you. How are things going?" he asked.

Emma felt a jolt of relief. "I called you before."

"Yeah, I just got in. One of the guys needed some help with some pretty tricky case law, and as usual, I got elected," Steve told her.

"Steve, you're getting elected again, I'm afraid. I'm electing you. I really need you to help me, Steve. I'm almost despairing. Things have hit the ground floor and are heading for the basement, and I've got to get away. I need a whole new change of scenery. I've got to find my birth mother and I've got to find her quickly, and you told me—"

"And I meant it, Emma," Steve interjected, trying to calm her down in his most reassuring manner.

Emma didn't skip a beat. "And what are we talking about in terms of time, Steve? You've got to tell me because my life is upside down. I left home, I got a job that sucks, and I'm living here, all alone, in this two-family apartment that is nothing to write home about. You've got to help me, Steve," Emma pleaded.

Walsh was startled at the breaking news. "What about school? What about Central? You're still there, I hope," Steve questioned her.

Emma held her breath a moment before telling him. "I suspended my semester. It can be reinstated if I want, but for the moment, you're talking to a working girl, a working girl who knows she's made some mistakes along the way," Emma confessed.

Steve became really worried. "Why don't you go home? Why don't you go back to your dad's?" he sincerely advised.

Emma bristled at the thought. "You don't know what he's been like and what it's been like for me living there. 'Emma, do this,' 'Emma, do that,' 'Emma, cook dinner,' 'Emma, take out the trash,' 'Emma, wait on me,' 'Emma, you're useless,' 'Emma, I wish you were Liz,'" she blurted.

Steve couldn't believe what he was hearing. "He really said that to you? He really said he wished you were Liz?" Steve interrogated.

Emma was ready for him. "Not exactly in those words all the time, Steve, but did you ever know what it was like to always hear how absolutely fantastic your sibling was without ever hearing something good about yourself from someone who really mattered? Well, that's it in a nutshell. Liz is wonderful, Emma is below grade. And why do you think it's like that over here? Because Liz is really their child, and Emma is adopted, and that's how it's been my entire life, and now I know I have to find my birth mother. I have to have my own identity. I have to hear from her that I count, that I'm important. Don't you understand?" she cried out to him.

Steve felt her anguish and thought he understood her pain. "You know, Emma, I'm the second son to the Walshes. My older brother, Jerry, well, he's several years older, and he's the apple of their eye—my parents, I mean. Jerry is already a doctor. He's a neurosurgeon down at Johns Hopkins. I spent a long, lonely childhood myself, hearing how Jerry walked on water. So I kind of know where you're coming from, and I am going to help you, and I do have some good news for you. So you really caught me at a good time," he announced.

Emma's heart pounded inside her chest. "Please, Steve, be on the level with me. Don't build my hopes up only to get punched in the mouth. What is it, Steve? What are you talking about?" she excitedly asked him.

Steve really wanted to help her. "I'll have some good news in a few days. I spoke to my uncle, the one who controls everything. Luckily, he likes me. I'm his favorite. Anyhow, that's one that Jerry lost, I guess."

"Go on, go on," Emma pushed him. "So I talked to Uncle Bob, and he said no problem, he'll have your complete file in a day or two. He just needs to know a little bit about your situation, like time and place of birth, where did the Molloys get you, what adoption agency, things like that. We tell him the story, he gives you the file. It's as simple as that. You do know some of that stuff, don't you, Emma?" Steve asked.

"Yes, I overheard a few things growing up," Emma replied.

Steve was elated. "Great. So go ahead. You start spilling, and I'll start writing, and maybe we can write in a happy ending together," Steve coaxed her, thinking of the possibilities that a union with Emma could bring and hoping that such a union could take place.

XI

Almost a week went by, and Emma's father was becoming desperate about getting his youngest daughter to come home. Days felt like weeks, and with each passing day, Tom feared that his chances for ever getting her back grew smaller while his hopes grew fainter.

Early that evening, he came out from the kitchen, drink in hand, and picked up the phone in the living room by his favorite chair. He took a drink and thought of Emma and began to cry, so he put the phone back down. Deep in his heart, he knew he had taken her for granted all these years, but then he thought back to when his son died, and he started to try to rationalize his behavior against his loss. But the old arguments that had swept through his mind quickly faded into obscurity, and he finally admitted to himself that one thing had nothing to do with the other. He looked up and tried to pray but only felt too unworthy to even attempt a prayer. He realized now that he really blew it with Emma and cried out in frustration and anguish for a second chance.

Tom took a stiff drink, trying to rally his courage, and picked up the phone again and dialed his daughter's number.

"Hello," Emma answered, sounding like she was nearly exhausted.

"Hello, sweetheart, this is your father. I'm calling to see how you're doing," he said to her before even attempting to get down to business. Emma was happy to hear from him.

"Hello, Daddy," she replied in her best girlish way.

Tom felt like there might be some hope. He conjured up a smile and tried to put forth his best salesmanship. "You know, dear, you have been missed by you know who, and I'm not just saying it because the kitchen's a mess or because I don't have any clean clothes to wear or the refrigerator is empty. No, I'm not saying it for any of those reasons, Emma."

"Father, are you all right?" Emma questioned, showing legitimate concern for him.

Tom paused for a moment. "Yes, no, I don't know, but I didn't call you to alarm you. I called you to see how you're doing. It isn't about me, it's about you. So tell me, how is Emma doing?" he tactfully asked her.

Emma was a little surprised at all the attention, but she liked it; she knew it felt good, especially coming from him. "Well, Daddy, I'm all right, I guess. The O'Learys treat me very nicely, they're very good, but to tell you the truth, it's just not the same. I mean, sure, they're wonderful and all that, and they are, but they're just not family. I wish I could—"

"You wish you could what, dear?" Tom anxiously interrupted.

"I wish I could have it both ways, I guess. I wish I could have something like this but with my own family, that's it," she said, having trouble getting the words out.

Tom saw his opening. His heart raced for a moment, but he remained calm. "Emma, you can. You can have it both ways. Trust me," he assured her in his most convincing voice.

"I believe you, Father. I'm sure the kitchen's a mess and all that, but I believe you. I believe that you actually do miss me...me, your daughter, not me, your cleaning service," she replied, laughing a little to herself over the way she said it.

Tom was delighted. He joined in with the laugh and then picked up his glass and took a fast sip. Courage, he told himself. Emma sensed it was time for her to make her statement.

"Father, I'm sorry if I hurt you. I know you want me to come home. I've had a good chance to think things over. I admit that my current situation isn't the greatest. It isn't the worst, but it isn't the best either," she put forth, trying to hold her position in the negotiations.

"Sweetheart, none of that matters. You tried something, you got some results from the trial, you can now decide what's best for you. I know that. That's how it should be," Tom coached her.

Emma was impressed with the way he was handling it. "You're right, Daddy, and thanks. So although it's not my final decision, I'm pretty close to it, I think, and here it is. I'm probably willing to come home, provided a couple of things are settled. Number one, things don't improve over the next few days at my job. Number two, the O'Learys don't mind me leaving. I mean, after all, I did sign a rental paper with them. And number three—and you have to promise me on number three—so here's the big one, Daddy. Number three, I get treated the same as Liz all the time from now on, no exceptions. You must promise. You have to say it," Emma insisted, wiping away a small tear under her eye.

Tom was relieved. It could have been a hell of a lot worse, he thought to himself. "Okay, sweetheart. You have my word. It won't be Liz and then you somewhere back there anymore. It will be you and Liz, and it will be like that forever, I promise," he solemnly said.

Emma was satisfied by the sound of his voice. "I believe you, Father," she said, closing the deal in her mind.

"Thank you, Emma," Tom sincerely replied, causing her to experience an inner joy that she had never felt before, an inner joy that was now enabling her to easily laugh.

"But I still have to credit about five percent to the kitchen's a mess, to you don't have any clean clothes to wear, and to the high likelihood that the refrigerator is empty, if that's okay with you, Daddy," she said, laughing into the phone, feeling that the world was suddenly a better place.

Tom was laughing right along with her. "I'm very happy to hear that, Emma," he told her.

Emma wanted to keep the good feeling going. She quickly thought about his drinking but decided not to address it. That would probably only be empty promises, promises he probably could not keep. "I've just got a few loose ends to take care of, Daddy, and I'll—"

"You take care of whatever you need to take care of. I'll be waiting for you when you're ready. Good night, sweetheart. I love you," he gently assured her before hanging up the phone.

Emma put the phone down and went into the bedroom and lay on top of the bed. What a day it had been, she thought to herself. First, Jenny quitting her job over at the diner. Then Joe insinuating that she should get a little friendlier to him, backed up by Matilda suggesting the same thing. It never ends over at that place, Emma thought to herself. And finally, this—her father coming to her on her terms just in the nick of time and on so many levels. Emma looked up at the ceiling and saw in her mind how she could have it all.

The O'Learys, well, that one would be easy. Rose O'Leary had practically adopted her herself, Emma thought. No, there shouldn't be any problem there. And the job... Emma pictured herself stringing Joe along, short term only, before walking out on him. That felt good, she conjured up in her mind. That left only one other thing, finding my birth mother, Emma told herself, getting up from the bed and pulling Steve's phone number out of her bag on the dresser. She went into the kitchen and picked up the phone and called Steve.

"Hello," he answered.

Emma sounded confident. "Hi, Steve, it's Emma. I'm calling to see how your uncle Bob is coming along. Does he need any more information or what?" she somewhat impatiently asked him.

Steve was happy she called. "I spoke to him two nights ago. He said he'd have it for me tomorrow midmorning, about eleven, at his office on College Point Boulevard. I was just going to call you. I can get it and meet you tomorrow at our bench if you like—you remember our bench at Central—or I can drop it off to you not this weekend but the following weekend because I'll be in Malba," he said.

Emma thought for a moment before answering. "Will Liz be with you on that weekend at Malba?" Emma intriguingly asked.

Steve laughed. "Well, you never can tell. I think she might, but I'm not sure. Who knows? She probably won't be, but then she's funny that way, even though we'd be chaperoned," he blurted out, trying to make Emma jealous.

Emma thought about her job and decided that she would pull the time, that she'd come in late. Joe wouldn't fire her now that Jenny was gone, she thought. Who would he flirt with?

"Steve, let's do this tomorrow. Meet me at the bench, say, noon. Can you make it by noon?" she asked, turning on the charm.

Steve felt a rush. "Noon, you've got it. Noon, our bench, tomorrow, with folder," Steve coolly said, trying to impress her with his command of things.

"Thank you, Steve. Tomorrow then. I'll see you tomorrow at our bench," she said, leading him on just a little before hanging up the phone. Emma went into the bedroom and put on her best gray sweater, thinking of what she would say to Rose. She left the apartment and went down the stairs to the O'Learys' living room. Rose was sitting by herself on the sofa when Emma walked in.

"How are you, my dear?" Rose asked, looking up from her sewing. Emma smiled and sat down beside her. She was nervous, unsure how she was going to approach the subject.

"Cat got your tongue?" Rose quipped. Emma paused and then took hold of the old lady's hand.

"You're right, I guess it does," Emma slowly responded.

Rose sensed that something wasn't quite right. "Well, go on, child. I've got the time if you need to talk about something. Please, Emma, tell me what's wrong," Rose encouraged. Emma's confidence began to build.

"I do have something on my mind, Rose. It's the job— no, I guess it's really a lot more than that. It's my dad. He called a little while ago. He really didn't sound so good. He wants me to come home," Emma told her, hoping for the best. Rose wasn't the least bit surprised.

"Your father needs you, but you already know that now, don't you?" Rose guided her in a motherly way.

Emma nodded. "I've known it all along. I just felt that there was this other thing I had to do given the situation," Emma tried to explain.

Rose continued trying to help her. "What situation might you be talking about, Emma, if you don't mind my asking?" Rose said.

Emma felt more at ease with her. "The situation is two-fold. Oh, I know my father needs me, and I know I really need to go to him and help him. But there's another side to the coin that, well, I'd rather not talk about," she said, sounding somewhat mysterious.

Rose was enamored with her answer. "Well, that's okay, Emma, if you really don't want to talk about it. But then again, sometimes it's better to get things off one's chest. If you feel it might be helpful to talk about your part two, well, I give you my word that whatever you tell me will go no farther than these four walls. And besides, Jack's asleep. He wasn't feeling so great, so he went in and lay down. I checked on him a few minutes ago, he's out like a light," Rose assured her.

Emma thought to herself it might not be so bad to get a trustworthy friend's opinion. "Rose, my part two, as you call it, is the fact that I'm adopted. That's probably the cause for more than half my problems. My sister, Liz, well, she's natural-born. She's a little older than me and, well, you see, she was always put up on a pedestal, while I was always, well, I was always treated like last week's cold pizza, especially by my father," Emma revealed, feeling unsure of whether she should continue talking.

Rose put her hand on her shoulder and pulled her toward her and gave her a hug. "I see. That's a lot for anyone to have to go through. And I suppose that led to leaving home, the diner job, your—"

"My mistakes," Emma interrupted.

Rose smiled. "Yes, those too. But don't despair, never give up," Rose encouraged.

Emma felt like she should keep going. "That's what I'm trying to do, not give up, I mean. I know what I need to do with my father, especially after this phone call. But there's more, more that I need to do, and that's the part two. I need to find my birth mother. I need to fill in the blank spaces of who I am, where did I come from, is my birth mother alive, is she okay, or is she poor and destitute and in a great need of help? I need to find out what's going on on the other side of this dark, black wall that keeps me separated from knowing her and knowing about myself at the same time. Rose, that's the main thing I need to do for myself. I need to find out the truth before I can really go on, before I can really live again or do anything of consequence," Emma said, coming to grips with her own life.

Rose leaned back on the sofa and looked up toward the ceiling, picturing her own daughter Kelly in her mind before turning back to Emma. "I feel for you, you know that, don't you?" Rose said. Emma nodded at her. "I feel for you because of your situation and also because of the difficulties you will face in trying to gain access to your mother. The government has made it all but impossible for you or anyone else to get the information they need to complete the circle. Oh, they'll give you their reasons for the roadblock, they'll talk about privacy, and then they'll tell you that they feel bad for you but that there's nothing that can be done. They'll give you the usual runaround, but nevertheless, that doesn't help you. It only keeps you in the dark. And here we are, living in the modern world, and they run things as if we were still in the Dark Ages," Rose empathized.

"I might have a way to get some information on my mother," Emma said.

Rose didn't hear her. "The only thing you need to be careful about, Emma, is that your father doesn't find out. It would probably hurt him, it could even kill him depending on what sort of a man he was. It could be a terrible blow to his ego. You know how men are. I'd be a bit careful with that one if I were you," Rose coached her.

Emma repeated her statement. "Rose, I might have a way to get some information on my mother. I have a friend who has some pretty good family connections. This guy kind of likes me. Anyhow, his uncle is some big-shot in Queens, and he told my friend he'd pick it up for him, that he'd get my case file," Emma anxiously explained.

Rose smiled at her. "Well, I always knew you were a bright, smart girl. You've got the idea, all right. It's all about connections. You've got to know how to get them and you've got to know how to use them before you can go anywhere in this world. I'm happy to see you're using your head because that's the only way you'll get to first base with anything like this," Rose exclaimed, patting Emma on the knee.

"What if I stay here with you a little longer until I clear up this chapter of my life, and then I go home to my father and do what I've got to do?" Emma asked, feeling confident she would get the right answer. Rose laughed a little to herself. "Well, if you're worried about the rent and getting out of the rental agreement or anything of that nature, don't you worry one iota, my child. Jack and I will be fine. We'll miss you but we'll be fine. It won't be too long before we'll be joining our Kelly in heaven. We're not dependent on the rent at all. So don't you worry about it. It's as if you hit the Irish sweepstakes when you first came through that door," Rose said, laughing out loud.

Emma was really touched. She took hold of the woman's hand and leaned toward her and kissed her on the cheek. "I'll never forget you and Jack as long as I live," Emma graciously told her, rising to her feet. She bent down, and warmly hugged her friend. "God bless you, Rose," she whispered and then she stood up, turned, and went back up the stairs.

The next day turned out to be nice and sunny. Emma sat in the front of the bus as it made its way along Kingsley Boulevard toward Central College. She looked at her watch. It was almost noon. She pictured the bench where she was to meet Steve in her mind and thought to herself that she was

141

halfway home to finding her mother. The driver pulled up to the stop, and Emma got off and crossed over to the campus. It felt funny arriving at that late an hour, she thought as she walked up the hill toward the bench.

"Hello, Emma, I missed you in class," a young woman called over to her.

Emma waved but kept on moving. "Hi, Rachael. Something came up. I'll be back soon. Talk to you then," Emma responded, picking up her pace. Finally, she saw the bench and felt relieved. Steve was sitting there, waiting for her.

"Hi, beautiful," Steve called out as she approached. Emma was somewhat startled by his comment.

"Hello, Steve," she cautiously answered, not wanting to let things get out of hand with him.

"Come on over and sit down. I won't bite," Steve playfully said, feeling like he was in the driver's seat. "I've got your complete history, from the time you entered planet Earth until the time you became daughter number two at Molloy House," he said, trying to be funny.

Emma didn't laugh. She nervously tried to smile, but the situation was too important to her for playtime. "Well, aren't you going to give it to me?" she anxiously asked, sitting down next to him.

Steve handed her the file that was wrapped in a white plastic bag. Emma pulled the weighty manila envelope out and opened it. She began to glean through the documents but then decided there was just too much there, and perhaps it wasn't the right time and place with Steve sitting next to her.

"Aren't you going to ask me anything?" Steve said.

Emma kept staring down. "Did you read any of this?" Emma asked him.

Steve inched a little closer. "I skimmed it to make sure that you weren't wasting a trip. I didn't want you to get your hopes up and then find out that Uncle Bob delivered plenty of nothing, so yes, I went through it. It seems like you're in luck. Your mother is a local woman, local in terms of the New York region, that is, if God willing she's still alive. I hope so for your sake, but I don't know the answer to that one, Emma. If I did, I would tell you," Steve imparted.

Emma looked somewhat perplexed. "What do you mean by New York region? What can you tell me about where she's from? She's not from Queens, is she?" Emma prodded.

"No, in a way, you're lucky. She wasn't a Queens girl. Apparently, her roots were in Fishkill. Do you know where that is?" Steve asked.

Emma drew a blank. "Why don't you tell me?" she answered.

Steve was getting somewhat frustrated with her demeanor, expecting to see a little friendlier gratitude out of her. "Fishkill is near Beacon. Do you know where that is?" he postured.

"Beacon, why, no. I never heard of it. Can you give me some better clues? I'm not exactly a triple A road map. Name something that makes sense, Steve. Come on, this is important," she said, getting a little flustered.

Steve moved back from her a few inches, seeing that things weren't going according to plan. A moment went by as he searched his mind for the answer. "Emma darling, did you ever hear of West Point? You must have heard of that one," he unwittingly said while losing his patience with what was transpiring.

Emma slapped his shoulder. "Stop making fun of me," she scolded, trying to sound a little playful herself.

Steve paused a moment and then began to laugh. "I don't get this much aggravation from your sister. I guess she's just a little smarter than you," he told her.

Emma paid no attention. "So where in relation to West Point is this mystery place, as you portray it, is this Fishkill?" she cagily asked him.

Steve could see he pushed things too far bringing up Liz. "West Point is the west bank, and Fishkill is practically the east bank, and I don't mean Paris. I mean the Hudson River. You did hear of that one," he teased her, trying to sound funny.

Emma looked at him and smiled a flirty smile. "I'm not stupid. Of course, I know it's not the Paris west bank, you idiot," she countered, turning away and looking across the lawn at a young couple walking together.

Steve became more forceful. "The file is pretty complete. Like I said, I skimmed it and I think it will give you all the answers you could have hoped for. I don't think that Uncle Bob screwed up, the man's a freaking genius," Steve boasted, trying to regain control.

Emma gently put her hand on the side of his face. "Thank you, Steve, my hero," she said, moving in closer to give him a kiss on the cheek. Steve put his hand behind her head and pulled her closer to kiss her on the mouth. "Steve, I just wanted to thank you, that's all," Emma insisted, pulling back and away from him.

Steve felt a jolt inside and quickly became embarrassed. "What's wrong with you?" he angrily demanded.

Emma took a deep breath. "Look, Steve, I really appreciate all you've done for me, but you're a friend, Steve, that's all. You're my sister's boyfriend, too, hello. That makes a big difference. It's a big deal. She's not my favorite person in the world, but she is my sister, and I'm not about stealing her boyfriend. You never know, you may end up being the only boyfriend that nasty sister of mine ever gets," Emma ridiculed.

Steve saw that his chances with her were an illusion. He got up from the bench and began to quickly pace in front of her. "Emma, I hate to break your little bubble, but you don't mean anything like that to me either. I'm not trying to chase after you, so just get that out of your head. I'm very happy with Liz. Liz and I are more alike, more socially compatible, more socially cohesive, more with the same likes and dislikes," he quickly invented, stumbling over some of the words.

Emma didn't want to push the issue; she didn't want to turn him into an enemy. She got up and stood next to him and put her hand on his shoulder. "It's okay, Steve. I'm sorry for some of the things I said. I want us to be friends. I'm glad you're happy with Liz, really, I am. If you weren't, who knows, I'm sure I could probably get interested. So let's just leave it at that, let's just leave here the way we came here. Let's leave here as friends," she said, taking hold of his hand and squeezing it.

Steve began to simmer down. "You're right, Emma, I'll be okay, and so will you once you find your mother. Good luck to you, Emma, and call if there's anything else I can do for you. And remember, mum's the word," he said and then he kissed her on the cheek and turned and walked away. Emma stood there and watched him, expecting him to turn and wave, but he never did; he just kept walking.

Late that afternoon, Tom Molloy returned home to what he thought would be another dreary night in an empty house. He went into the living room, took off his coat, and sat down in his easy chair, thinking about the Peters case at the office, sketching out arguments to make in his mind on behalf of his firm's client. The house seemed unusually empty, and for a moment, he just leaned back, closed his eyes, and tried to relax. He thought about getting up for a drink but then fought the urge, believing that Emma would be home any day now, and perhaps he could curtail some of the drinking. He sat there motionless and began to drift off just as Emma tiptoed down the stairs and quietly walked over in front of his chair. A moment went by, and Tom opened up his eyes to the vision he had been longing for.

"Emma," he cried out as he started to get up to greet her.

Emma smiled and gently pushed against his shoulder. "Don't bother getting up, Father. I'm so very happy to see you," she told him, bending down to kiss him on the cheek.

Tom was delighted, and a big, wide smile covered his face. "You're looking fantastic, Emma. I'm so very happy to see you. In fact, I was just thinking about you. Yeah, I told myself to take a pause on my next trip to the bar because Emma would be coming home soon, and I wanted to get in shape and stay in shape for the big event," he said, allowing a little humility to come through.

"I'm sure everything is going to be all right, Daddy. Now let me tell you about me, about what's going on—"

"I'm all ears, I'm dying to hear, sweetheart," Tom cut in.

"Things are good, and they're going to get even better, Father. From now on, you're looking at the next great Molloy lawyer. That's right. I'm focusing on law or prelaw courses for the time being. I talked to a Miss Emerson today in Central's administrative offices. I explained to her that I had been a bit lost, not really focused on what I wanted to pursue in life, but that now, after much soul-searching, I wanted to follow in my father's footsteps and take up law."

"What did Ms. Emerson say?" Tom anxiously asked her.

Emma's face lit up. "She told me that she'd have to look at my transcript before she could—"

"And did she?" Tom eagerly interrupted.

"Well, yes, Daddy, I'm just getting to that. She reviewed the transcript for about fifteen minutes while I sat in the office."

"And then what?"

"And then she told me that she noticed I had a very high writing aptitude."

"Go on, go on," Tom cut in again, hardly able to contain himself.

"And then she told me that in her professional opinion, she had probably never seen a better fit as far as career choice goes given the writing and the entrance exam scores I had gotten when I took my SATs back in high school," Emma told him.

"Did she have anything to say about your recent exodus de campus?" Tom inquired, trying to sound funny with his phrasing.

Emma laughed. "No, Daddy, she didn't. It didn't even really come up. Not really. I mean, she touched on it, but I just explained that I was having an early midlife crisis regarding career interests and all that, and she simply answered me with a weighty-sounding 'What else is new these days?'"

Tom reached for her hand and gently squeezed it. "Well, that's all that matters as far as Ms. Emerson goes. Now less of her and more of you. What are your plans? What are you thinking about in terms of getting your four-year degree and then selecting a law school?" Tom questioned.

Emma reached down and put her hand on his shoulder. "Daddy, this is going to be easy because I'm really focused. I figure to finish this semester and then transfer to Columbia for the undergrad and then attend their law school, just like you know who," she said, removing her hand and sitting down on the sofa.

Tom had pretty much been expecting this. "All right then, it's settled. You get the grades, I'll get the money for our little venture. And, Emma, I'm just sorry we didn't have this conversation a long time ago, but we can't relive the past. Hopefully, we can learn from it. And just one other thing, are you back here to stay starting, say—"

"Yes, Daddy, I'm back. I talked it over with the O'Learys. No hard feelings on their part, Daddy. I guess I just got lucky on that one. Mrs. O'Leary thought it was all for the best, so things are okay on that front," Emma relayed, getting up from the sofa and taking a step closer to him. "So let me just run upstairs and take care of a couple of things, and then I'll come right back down and get dinner started. I checked earlier and I can come up with a nice lasagna tonight before I hit the stores for us tomorrow," she said, heading toward the staircase. Then she stopped in her tracks and turned back to him and ran over and kissed him on the cheek before running up the stairs. Tom sat there in his chair, somewhat bewildered, but more than that, he sat there extremely happy for a change.

The following morning, Emma walked up the street and waited for the bus. She thought about how well it had gone with her father and telling him about her school plans and how for the first time in her adult life she felt on equal footing with Liz. And then she chuckled to herself over her father telling her at dinner just how he had decided to go into law after first striking out in a mechanical engineering curriculum and just how much in common his story made it seem. The bus pulled up and Emma got on. She looked down the aisle and saw Kate Brown waving to her.

"Come on, Emma, come over here," Kate called out to her. Emma made her way and sat down beside her.

"Nice to see you on the early bus again. I hope you're not just passing through but might be staying a while," Kate said, obviously happy to see her friend.

Emma laughed, placing her bag on her lap. "Not to tell you I didn't try would be a lie. I did try to make it on my own, but the entire world blew up on me. I got jilted at this job I dug up. I mean, the owner was an absolute pig—"

"Tried hitting on you," Kate cut in, only half-asking.

Emma nodded. "You said a mouthful. The girl who trained me quit just before I did. Anyway, my father began to fall apart with me being gone and all. I thought I was going to be told that he woke up dead one morning. And to top it all off, I found myself to be utterly freaking bored with nothing on the horizon to stimulate my brain. And so, with all that said, here I am headed back to class, only this time I'm going to class with a plan," Emma revealed.

Kate couldn't resist. "Sounds serious. Let's hear about the plan. Tell me you've got a chance to study in Europe or something like that provided your father gets to tag along," Kate taunted.

Emma shook her head. "No, it's nothing like that. I'm just going to really buckle down and then get out of this flea-bag school and transfer to Columbia at the end of the semester or next semester the latest. Then once I'm over there, I'm going to do a kick-ass job in undergrad and then go to their law school. And my father is backing me. He's actually on my side," Emma told her.

Kate paused a moment. "And where does he go once you go? Columbia isn't exactly right around the corner," Kate nudged.

"We didn't talk about that, but if he wants to, he can move into the city near the campus. I will take care of him, I mean I won't just walk out on him. Not after last night. He's backing me, I mean all the way, so I'll stand by him," Emma confided just before the bus pulled up to their stop.

Kate was genuinely happy for her. "Well, it sounds like a plan, Emma. And I hope it works out for you the way you want it to," she told her as they got up to get off the bus.

They exited the vehicle and then crossed the street to the campus side. "Give me a minute, I need to mail something," Emma told her friend, pulling an envelope postmarked "Fishkill" from her bag and dropping it into the mailbox.

"More tuition money," Kate quipped as Emma caught up to her.

"No, just the check for that study cruise to Europe you spoke about earlier," Emma shot back, causing Kate to laugh.

"I knew it. Aren't you the lucky one?" Kate bantered while the two young women walked off to class.

Before they reached the building, Emma stopped and turned to her friend. "I've got to ask you something, Kate, something personal."

Kate seemed surprised. "Go on, but I have to tell you, after my last piece of advice, you know, to leave home and all that, well, maybe I'm not the best person to ask. My track record isn't so hot," Kate replied as she started walking toward the door.

Emma called to her. "Kate, come back here a minute and forget about your track record. It wasn't your fault. It was my call and my bad luck, that's all. I never thought for a minute anything bad about you. You were a good friend trying to help, that's all. Besides, nobody's perfect. So come over here and listen. This is important," Emma pleaded.

Kate came right over to her. "Okay, I'm all ears, but we've got to get inside so—"

"So I'll give you the short version. It's my sister's boyfriend. He kind of likes me. How do I know that? He came on to me right over there at the bench. He showed up with some lame excuse and he—"

"I get it," Kate interrupted

Emma continued. "What should I do? I mean, should I tell my sister or what? I certainly am not interested in him."

"How do you and she get along?" Kate inquired.

"Like cats and dogs. It's not too good," Emma answered.

Kate looked up into the sky and took a deep breath. Then she looked Emma in the eye. "If it were me, I wouldn't say a thing. I'd make it real clear to the guy, though, that he had better bug off. But as to your sister, the hell with her. What did she ever do for you except tick you off? Now come on and let's get inside," Kate said as she started walking away again.

Emma thought to herself that perhaps Kate was right on this one as she caught up to her and they entered the building.

That afternoon saw a bit more hustle and bustle at the Columbia campus than usual with students and faculty hurrying about, as if the future of Western civilization hung in the balance. Liz walked out onto the lawn, taking a short-cut to get back to her apartment for a date with Wilson's Corporate Case Studies Journal and maybe a glass of wine or two.

"Hello over there, beautiful," a familiar voice rang out, stopping her in her tracks. A small, hopeful smile covered her face.

"And who might you be? Could you be Sir Lancelot?" she called to him, turning around one hundred and eighty degrees.

Steve came running up to her. "Yes, my dearest Guinevere, it is I, your knight in shining armor," Steve came back with, playing along with her. He put both hands on her shoulders and then stepped back and bowed at the waist.

Liz had had enough. "All right, what's up with you? You're acting awfully stupid. You must be trying to get on my good side for not taking me to the Met, and I do so love those Impressionists. I see that—"

"You see that I am hopelessly in love with you," Steve flirted.

Liz wasn't buying it. She still believed there was something going on between him and her sister. "Well, if you love me so much, here carry my books for me. They're getting heavy, and I have to rest up. I've got a lot of important things to do and I can't burn all my energy on anything so trite as carrying schoolbooks. So here, you take them," she ordered, handing two heavy textbooks to him and then turning to walk away.

Steve followed right behind. "Oh, come on, Liz, stop breaking my chops. So we missed the museum. So what? There will be other museums, other Impressionists, other French... I don't know what," he exclaimed.

Liz seemed a little happier. She felt she was taking control. "You say that now because you know I'm mad at you. You know you're in the doghouse and you know you're not coming out anytime soon. I don't think it was very nice. And I won't think it was very nice for at least twenty-four hours or more, who knows? But you can call then, and we'll see," she told him, laying it on really thick.

Steve's face dropped. He was really flustered. He thought of Emma and how that had failed so miserably. He wasn't about ready to go 0 for two so fast. "Liz, what's the matter? We missed one thing. I'm sorry. I had to go to Queens. My uncle Bob is dying. He's a sick man. I didn't want to tell you because it's pretty gruesome. He's got prostate cancer, and it's spread to his brain," he mistakenly said.

"Prostate doesn't have anything to do with the brain, you idiot. The only thing spreading around here is the spreading going on inside your head between your two little brain cells," Liz snapped at him while trying to decide just how far she was going to push.

Steve thought about what he said and became embarrassed but then tried to turn it to his advantage. "Okay, Liz, you got me on that one. I admit it. I embellished it a little, but the old man is really sick. I couldn't take you there because he is pretty bad, and I'm his favorite nephew and I wasn't going to do anything to get him upset. He's worth a fortune, and that wouldn't be too smart, if you get my drift," Steve countered.

Liz became really angry with him. "So you did it for him. You couldn't—"

"I couldn't miss being there. I've got to tell you something about me and him. We've always been really close, and in this case, I had to put him first. No surprises, no stress, no strain. I just had to put him first. I didn't have a choice. He may not have long to go," Steve insisted.

"All right then, I suppose I'll have to cut the twenty-four hours in half."

"Why not try cutting it into less than that?" Steve romantically said, throwing his arms around her and giving her a big kiss on the mouth. "There, that's more like it, Lady Guinevere," he softly whispered in her ear, wondering if there would be a second chance for him with her sister.

"Well, if you're a good boy, Lancelot, there might be more where that came from," Liz said as her resistance began to crumble. Steve looked at her and smiled, but Liz didn't smile back. "But don't get too cozy with me just now, for your sentence has yet to be carried out. It's ten hours for you, and then you may seek my hand," she said, laughing delightedly to herself at the sound of her own voice.

Steve started to chuckle along with her. They began walking in the direction of her apartment. A few moments went by, and they walked past the remaining college building. Liz couldn't stop thinking about him and the possibility of his leaving her for Emma; she couldn't stop picturing him passing Emma that note at her mother's after-service gathering at the Red Fox restaurant. Liz wanted to find out more from him; she wanted the truth, but she just didn't know how to approach the subject. For some reason, Steve did it for her.

"These books are getting heavy. Can you take them for the next block? And oh, by the way, I forgot to tell you, but I bumped into your sister when I was at Central a while back. Yeah, I was over there trying to help my sister, Mary, who might end up going there. Do you believe that? I'm over trying to help my sister, and I bumped into your sister. What a coincidence."

"What made you think of that?" Liz questioned, slowing down her walk.

Steve couldn't help himself. "Oh, I don't know. I guess it must have been our talking about Uncle Bob. You see, he really likes my kid sister, Mary, and Mary has a bit of a learning disability, and I found out that Uncle Bob wants her to be able to go to college, and Central is probably the only place on earth that will take her and—"

"And you just happened to bump into my sister while you were there," Liz interjected, feeling the hairs on the back of her neck stand up.

"Yeah, that's right. She was out on their main lawn by the administration building where I had to go to dig up the scoop for Mary, and presto, like magic, there she was," Steve tried to carefully explain.

Liz was becoming unglued at the precision of his recollection. "Why are you telling me this?" she impatiently asked, not really wanting to hear another word while at the same time not wanting to miss a thing.

Steve could see that he really screwed up trying to get information from Liz about Emma. "I'm telling you because I wanted you to know that you're the prettiest girl in New York, much better than her, but like I said, Uncle Bob got it into my head. Anyway, it looks like Mary is going to go there next fall. So thank Emma for me because when I met her there, she pointed out the building for me to go into. That's all, just thank her for me," Steve told her, trying to sound as innocent as possible as they reached the front door of Liz's building.

"I'd ask you up but I've got a lot of work to go over, Steve. However, I'll be free tomorrow after four, if you'd like to stop back then," Liz suggested, trying to camouflage her inner turmoil.

Steve kissed her and then smiled. "Okay, my Guinevere, four it is. I'll let you go for now but I will return, hence yonder, at tomorrow's four. Happy studying, and I'll see you then. We can hang out at Frank's or something," he said, trying to sound as carefree as possible, as though nothing happened.

Liz watched while he turned and walked back toward the college. She pictured Emma in her mind and thought to herself just what it would take in this war with her sister, who was obviously well on her way to stealing Steve away from her.

It was a little after the lunch crowd had begun emptying out when Tom Molloy stopped in at his favorite New York restaurant.

"Good afternoon, Mr. Molloy, and welcome back to Le Chic. So nice to see you again, sir. Your usual table is available," Tony said, sounding like the most competent maître d' in New York.

"That will be fine, Tony. Send over my usual scotch and—"

"I remember, sir. I'll have it for you in a moment," Tony cut in as they walked over to the table, and then Tony seated his guest.

"I'll order after my friend arrives," Tom told him, beaming with a smile.

"Nice to see that smile on your face, Mr. Molloy. Things must be going well for you. I'm very happy to see that and to see you back here," he warmly said.

"Nice to see you too, Tony," Tom replied, and then Tony turned and left him. Tom stared out the window, reflecting on how things had turned around so much for the better now that Emma was back and he and Emma had become friends.

"Hello, Tom," Brian Toddman's familiar voice called to him. "I guess they'll let anyone into Le Chic these days," Brian said, joking around.

Tom laughed. "I guess you're right. They let you in, didn't they?"

Brian broke out with a loud laugh. "No argument there, old friend. Now let me sit down and join you, and get you to explain to me what it is that accounts for that mystical glow I saw on your face when I first walked over here. Tell me McManus Engineering is in breach of something even more costly than the Miller's Point nuclear power station, and you can even get me to pay for lunch," Brian proposed, laughing to himself the whole time.

"No, it's even better than that. Emma. It's about Emma."

"Sounds important, go on," Brian encouraged.

Tom took a deep breath. "We've had our ups and down, but I've got to tell you that right now, I'm the happiest man on earth."

"Keep going, get to the bottom line. The suspense is killing me, old man," Brian bantered as the waiter showed up with Tom's drink.

"Anything for you from the bar?" the young man asked Brian, who waved him off.

"No, but give us at least a few minutes before we order. We've got some catching up to do," Brian told him, and then he left. "Okay, Mr. Molloy, now tell me, what's up? And don't spare me any of the details. I'm just in the frame of mind for a good story with a happy ending. I haven't had one of those since we bailed out McManus the last time," Brian said, feeling really happy for his friend.

Tom took a sip and put the glass down. "Emma's going to go to law school. She's finishing up at Central, she'll transfer to Columbia for undergrad, and then she'll knock them dead at the law school. For Emma, it's always been a matter of her finding herself, of finding out what she wanted to do. It always seemed to be difficult for her, but I really believe that now she has finally found it, and it is law," Tom proudly proclaimed.

Brian was delighted. "Maybe I should have that drink after all," he quipped, picking up his napkin and holding it up for a toast in place of his drink.

"Thanks, Brian, it really means a lot to me seeing you here and being able to brag a little about my girl. I only wish we had become friends much sooner."

"Uh-uh, I wouldn't go there if I were you. Don't look back, look forward. Look forward and be thankful to heaven above that you have this moment, this time with her, and that you can enjoy it and that it will lead to something very productive in your daughter's life," Brian philosophized.

Tom nodded at him and then winked. "I can't tell you how happy I truly am, Brian. I've just got to tell you that it could have perhaps gone the other way. She could have left me. In fact, she did for a short time. She took an apartment, got a dumb local job, and nearly scared me half to death."

"Well, that's good to hear also. Look, you're out of the woods with her, Tom. She's already gone through that rebellion thing that all the kids do today, and in your case, no harm, no foul. So that's actually a good thing because the big emotional, life-changing episode that can really screw things up is in your rearview mirror, not in front of you. So nice going on that one, and if you see that kid, call him over because this really does call for a drink. I know what I'm talking about. I have two of my own, remember?" Brian saluted to his very good friend.

Tom called over the young waiter.

"Let me have a scotch and water, and hold the ice," Brian ordered, and then he turned his gaze back to Tom.

"So tell me, Brian, have you been following the story in the papers about the waterpower project?" Tom asked.

Brian laughed. "Oh, you mean the McManus, I don't ever do anything wrong, like cut critical structural corners, waterpower project. Is that the one you mean? That's what I thought we were getting involved with on the last go-round," Brian responded, chuckling to himself.

Tom began to laugh along with him. "Yeah, that waterpower project," Tom gleefully said, obviously enjoying the moment and where this was heading.

"Did they call you?" Brian asked, now sitting on the edge of his seat.

"Yup, they called," Tom answered.

"I thought they would by now, especially after the way we, uh, the way you plugged the hole in the prosecutor's case in the Miller's Point matter. Bravo and double bravo," Brian praised him.

Tom smiled with a more-than-just-content type of smile. "Are you interested in another go?" Tom asked his friend.

"Is the pope Catholic?" Brian quipped with a sly little laugh.

"Okay then."

"Did you push the fee?" Brian asked, upping the ante.

Tom laughed. "Same answer as to whether the pope is Catholic. The old man even brought it up himself this time, said he just had to have us. That was it. It was a done deal," Tom lauded. The waiter returned to the table and put Brian's drink down. "We'll order in a few minutes," Tom said to him, and the young man left.

Brian picked up his glass, took a deep breath, and made a toast. "Here's to the important things in life. Nice going on McManus and all that, but what I really want to say here, Tom, is that I wish you and Emma all the best, and I hope she fulfills your hopes for her to go on to law school. Congratulations, old friend, and Godspeed," Brian told him, and the two men clinked their glasses, truly enjoying their moment together.

XII

Almost two weeks went by. It was a Saturday afternoon. The streets were fairly well cleared from the snow that had fallen a few days earlier, and the hopefulness of spring was in the air. Liz walked up to the Molloy front door unannounced for a surprise visit home. She reached into her bag and pulled out her key. She turned the lock, opened the door, and walked inside, nearly slipping on the mail that was lying on the floor behind the mail slot in the door. She gathered herself, took a gasp of air, and proceeded into the living room to remove her coat.

The house appeared to be empty. Liz turned and went back to close the front door and collect the mail that was lying there. She reached down and picked up the several pieces and turned back toward the living room, casually browsing through what she now held in her hand. Strange, she thought to herself, viewing a return addressed envelope from Fishkill, New York, that was sent to Emma. Who could she possibly know in a town so far away? Liz thought, judging from its odd zip code. Liz wondered for a moment. Could it be some girl from school? But who in their right mind would come all the way down to Queens just to go to Central? she asked herself. And besides, the handwriting looked like that of a woman who was older, much older. No, it just didn't add up. Something was going on here, maybe something that would be worth her knowing about, she decided, as Emma came down the stairs and spotted her standing there.

"Well, this is certainly a pleasant surprise. What's the occasion?" Emma called to her, only partially hiding her disdain.

Liz turned and faced her. "Oh, it's you. How are you, Emma? I heard you left and came back or something. You got a job that crashed and you came running back home. Something like that, anyway," Liz ridiculed, trying to look not the least bit interested.

Emma walked up to her and took the mail out of her hand, but Liz grabbed it back. "Let me take it into Daddy. I want to surprise him," Liz said. Emma spotted the envelope from Fishkill. She quickly pulled it away from her. "What's the matter with you, Emma? What gives. I want to surprise Father. What's your problem? Do you have to take everything away from me? You tried stealing my boyfriend, now I see you're trying to steal my father as well. Let me tell you something, you little bitch. I'm just not going to let you get away with it. Now give me that before I—"

"Before you what? It's mine, get lost. He's in the den. You can go and take the rest of it into him, but you're not getting this. This belongs to me," Emma nervously yelled.

Liz took a step back. "What's in that, anyway? Who do you know in Fishkill? You're so stupid you probably don't even know where it is," Liz provoked her.

Emma's face turned red as she desperately tried to figure out in her mind if there was any way Liz could know anything about what was really going on. "Take a hike, Liz. He's inside like I told you," Emma screamed, trying to shake her loose.

Liz took a step closer to her. "Okay, for now. I'll go in and see him. But I'm not through with you regarding a certain Steve Walsh and how you lured him up to your stupid college and tried to seduce him," Liz accused her.

Emma tried to calm herself down. "Well, if you had what I have, you would already know that I didn't have to try to seduce him. He came after me without me even trying, probably because at the time, he was going out with you," Emma drilled her.

Liz became infuriated. "You're so full of it. You think you're so pretty, well, you're not. You're just a lazy little slut without any consideration for anybody other than yourself," Liz fired back.

Emma took a step back from her. She remained quiet, not quite knowing how much of this she was willing to continue going on with. She turned and started walking for the stairs when Tom suddenly entered the room, drink in hand.

"What a nice surprise to see you. How are you, Liz? And how are my two favorite girls getting along?" Tom happily asked, walking over and kissing Liz on the cheek.

Emma tucked her letter into her pant pocket and turned toward her father while Liz put her hand on his shoulder.

"I'm so happy to see you, Daddy," Liz replied, stepping back and handing him the mail.

"So tell us all the news. How are things going at Columbia?" Tom asked, walking over near his chair.

"I'm doing really well in school, Daddy, if that's what you're asking," Liz craftily said.

Tom detected a hint that something was wrong. "What else?" he demanded to know.

Liz saw this as her golden opportunity to really land one on Emma. "Well, now that you asked," she said, trying to play the role of the innocent, sweet, little thing. "Now that you asked, Daddy, it's been terrible. I lost my boyfriend

Steve, and it's been just awful," Liz revealed, playing it to the hilt.

Tom looked concerned. "Well, maybe that's not so bad, sweetheart. Maybe it's all for the best. Maybe you'll find someone a lot better real soon," Tom encouraged, taking a large gulp from his glass and then looking over at his other daughter. "Isn't that right, Emma?" Tom said, trying to find more compassion for Liz while taking still another drink.

"Father's correct, Liz," Emma told her right on cue.

Tom thought to himself for a quick topic changer. "Liz, I've got some interesting news for you," he said, getting into his chair.

Liz walked over and knelt down beside him. "Well, that's good. I could use some interesting news these days. So tell me, what's up, Daddy?" she asked.

Tom took a drink and put his glass down. "Your sister will be going to Columbia in the fall. She will be taking prelaw, just like you. I think it will be really good for the two of you both personally and professionally. Liz, you can show her the ropes up there, and, Emma, you and Liz can get some time together and hopefully go on to become really good friends."

Liz felt a surge of anger explode throughout her entire body, but she knew that somehow she had to mask it. "What a nice surprise," Liz said, gritting her teeth and swiftly rising to her feet.

Emma was somehow able to hold back the laughter. "I thought you'd like it, Liz. One good surprise, like your surprise visit, deserves another, as they say," Emma told her with an air of superiority.

Liz became infuriated, while Tom got up from his chair and stood next to Emma. "I think that with a little time, once you two get used to the idea, you'll see how nice the whole thing could work out. It could be a tremendous bene-fit to both of you," Tom said, putting his arm around Emma and motioning for Liz to come over and join in on the family hug. However, Liz was seeing nothing but red. She decided she'd roll the dice with her father.

"What I haven't made clear to you, Father, is that the reason I lost Steve is because he has been secretly seeing Emma. She got him to meet her over at her college. He told me so himself. And I believe him. There would be no reason for him to make anything like that up. That little sneak over there is a big fat zero when it comes to family loyalty, so you might as well know it also, Father, because I certainly do," Liz declared.

Tom was shaken to his core. He appeared to change color, becoming almost pale gray. He pulled his arm away from Emma and took a step back from her. "Emma, is this true? Is any of this possibly true?" Tom questioned her while starting to feel a definite shortness of breath from the stress of the situation.

Emma became frightened. She shook her head to tell him no but somehow couldn't muster any of the right words to come to her defense, much like when she was a young child those many years ago.

"See, Daddy," Liz jumped in. "See? I told you," Liz ada-mantly repeated.

Tom began feeling lightheaded, as if he were having a dizzy spell. "What the hell is the matter with you two?" Tom shouted, trying to overcome his condition.

"You can't send her to Columbia with me, Daddy. She'll drive me crazy if I have to see her walking around there on my ex-boyfriend's arm. She'd do it just to spite me, Father," Liz screamed at him.

Tom took a big gulp of air and turned to face Emma. "Aren't you going to say anything?" Tom interrogated her.

Emma paused for a moment, trying to steady herself. "It's not true, Father. None of it is true. She's crazy. I don't even like her boyfriend. He's not my type. I can do a lot better than Steve Walsh. I don't even think he's very good-looking, to tell you the truth," Emma said, rubbing it in on her sister.

"She's lying, Father," Liz screamed, nearly losing all sense of self-control.

Tom could feel his heart race. He made his way to his chair and sat down. "Leave him alone, Liz," Emma shouted as she went over to her father and put her hand on the top of his head. "Take it easy, Daddy," she gently said, picking up his nearly empty glass. "I'll make you a refill, you just sit here and take it easy, and let's all just try to forget the whole thing happened," Emma wisely counseled. She then walked into the kitchen to get him his drink.

"Daddy, I'm sorry you had to get dragged into this, but the fact remains that it's all true. So you can't possibly be even thinking about sending her to school with me. If she goes there, I don't know what I'll do," Liz threatened.

Tom appeared to be calming down a little. "Liz, she's your younger sister. One might think that you would take a little interest in her, wouldn't one?" Tom tried persuading.

Liz backed off some. "Father, I don't have anything against her other than what she's done behind my back with my ex-boyfriend. I would never have done anything like that to hurt her. And that's why she must have done it, to hurt me, because you heard her yourself say she doesn't give a hoot about him in the first place. She's just vindictive, Father, can't you see that?" Liz argued.

Tom could see that this was going nowhere except to a possible heart attack for himself. "All right Liz. I'll get over my attempts to reconcile the two of you, but the offer I gave Emma regarding her schooling still stands. I'll not take it away from her regardless of a missing boyfriend or two, and that's final," Tom said.

Emma returned with his drink. "Well, I hope I didn't miss anything, you two. Will you be staying for dinner, Liz?" Emma coyly asked, placing Tom's drink on the side table next to the mail.

Liz noticed the mail and remembered the letter from Fishkill. "Aren't you going to open—"

"And another thing," Tom interrupted, "I want you two to realize that I'm not as young as I used to be and that I probably can't take too many more battles around here like that last one. So I want you both to promise me that from now on, you'll both promise to do your fighting when I'm not around. Now go ahead, the two of you, promise," Tom said, looking straight at Liz.

Liz slowly nodded. "I promise, Daddy," she quietly said.

Emma volunteered right behind her. "And so do I, Father," she graciously told him. Tom felt relieved. "All right then, that settles matters," he said, leaning back in his chair and gazing up to the ceiling. "Now go ahead, the two of you, and leave me in peace for a little while," he told them.

Emma took hold of his hand. "I hope you're okay, Father. I'll be upstairs. I have to get back to my studying. I'll chat with Liz later, if she'd like," Emma said and then she instantly turned and walked toward the staircase to go back up to her room. She quickly ascended the stairs, walked into her bedroom, and pulled the letter out from her pocket.

She sat on the bed and began to tremble. She got up and closed the door to her room and returned to the bed and stood and stared at the letter lying before her on the bedspread. Emma's heart began to race from an anxiety—no, a fear that the contents inside the letter would tear her very soul apart. She sat on the bed and closed her eyes and whispered a prayer to God that she would now finally be getting the type of news she had hoped for, had longed for, her whole entire life. A tear gently rolled down the side of her face. Her hand began to shake, and she became light-headed in the surreal moment of a lifetime.

Finally, she went to her desk and got the letter opener. She sat back on the bed and told herself, "Okay; here goes." She carefully and meticulously dragged the opener across the top of the envelope, as though she were handling some ancient recently discovered manuscripts that contained all of the secrets of human history. Finally, the envelope was opened. Emma slowly reached in and placed the letter in between her fingers and gave it several gentle tugs, freeing the very paper her mother had touched from its container and letting her mother's own handwriting see the light of day before her very eyes. Then she carefully unfolded the precious object and held it in her hands before her and began to read.

Dear Emma,

I received your letter and, yes, I would certainly like to meet you. You have my address and perhaps you could arrange to come here and meet me at my home. I look forward to it. I should tell you that after Wednesday next, I will be away for a time. So for our get-together, I would suggest you plan for either before or after my trip, which could last several weeks, depending on circumstances. You can either call me or just come up and ring the bell. I wrote my number on the enclosed strip of paper so you can tuck it into your wallet and carry it with you. The easiest way to get here is the railroad from Grand Central up the Hudson River to the Beacon station where you can get a cab. It's only a short ride to the house.

Fondly,
Mary

Emma put the letter down beside her and got up and went over to the window. She looked out, feeling both a major sense of relief and an insatiable curiosity. The handwriting told her that her mother was somewhat on the older side, that she probably had her later in life. Emma also discerned that her long-held fears of her mother living in poverty were unfounded given the extent of the trip she was about to embark on, which gave her a real sense of relief. She looked out onto the quiet street, and a sense of calm overtook her. The most important question of them all had also been answered—the question of acceptance or rejection. Emma was not only just pleased with the resolution to some of the things that had nagged away at her for most of her life; she was truly joyful with an inner sense of peace that told her perhaps there really was a force for good, for what was right out there after all.

"Em, I thought we'd have time for our chat, you know, the one you told Father you wanted to have with me later," Liz said after quietly entering the room and looking down at the bed.

Emma was startled. "Don't you ever knock?" Emma exclaimed, turning and going over to the bed to block Liz's view.

"Father is going to be okay. He just got a little overexcited with the catfight. But I don't think it's critical. He'll be all right," Liz told her.

Emma slowly sat down on the edge of the bed, making sure to cover the letter. "So maybe you and I can bury the hatchet and possibly start over," Emma suggested in a very genuine way.

Liz appeared to be in an agreeable state. "You know, Emma, before I came up here, before Father got all worked up, I wanted to kill you for all the things you and Steve did to me. But after seeing him down there, after seeing him almost lose it and have a heart attack down there, I have since decided that it just isn't worth it. So there you have it. I do think it's possible for us to try to start over."

"No tricks?" Emma interrupted.

"No tricks on this end, Emma. And you?" Liz asked.

Emma breathed a sigh of relief. "Same here. No tricks, I promise. But there is just one other thing. You're okay with me going to Columbia?" Emma asked her, trying to diffuse what could be a major sticking point.

Liz took a step closer to her. "Columbia is fine with me, if that's what you really want," Liz said in a genuine sounding way.

Emma put out her hand as she got up from the bed, causing the letter to fall onto the carpet. She quickly went the few steps over to her sister and hugged her. "I hope we can truly be friends," Emma told Liz while trying to turn her line of sight away from the fallen letter.

Liz let go and smiled at her. "You know, Em, it hasn't been like this since we were kids. What happened to us? I guess I'll never know. I guess we'll never know. But one thing is for sure, I hope we can keep up all this goodwill, especially with Father the way he is. I hope we can keep it up," she repeated.

Emma turned and picked up the letter. She quickly folded it and placed it on the bed. "It's none of my business, but that must be Fishkill," Liz stated.

"Just a friend," Emma nervously responded, wondering just how much Liz got to see when she entered the room.

Liz sighed as though she was getting a little bored. "Oh well, I think I'll go downstairs and see how Father's doing. I'll see you down there later, and oh yes, Em, I'll be staying for dinner. I'll even help you put it together when you're ready, if you like," Liz told her and then she left the room.

Later that afternoon, Tom entered the dining room and sat down at the table. He put his glass of club soda down and called into the kitchen. "How's it coming in there, you two? I don't hear any kicking or screaming. Something must be wrong in that kitchen, but it's a wrong I can get used to," he said, amused at the way he put it.

"We're fine, Daddy," Liz called back.

Then Emma chimed in, "Everything's okay. We're just having a little girl talk, that's all. Dinner will be ready in a minute. I hope you're hungry," Emma called out to him before turning back to Liz. "I hope he's going to be all right. That was quite a scare before. I don't know what I would ever do if something like that—"

"You'd call the volunteer ambulance drivers, they're in the phone book and get them to send an ambulance," Liz instructed. Emma nodded at her. "Then you'd call me, and we'd handle it. But don't worry so much, Emma, because he's going to be just fine, especially now that we have our little truce. Things are going to be okay, you'll see. Now go in there at dinner and don't forget to tell him how we've made up and that we're both looking forward to you coming up to Columbia this fall," Liz said.

Emma smiled at her. "I'm really happy to hear that, Liz. I think it will be good. I think it will be fun," she told her as Liz began carrying the serving bowls out to the table.

"Nice to see you two actually getting along for once," Tom cajoled.

Liz put the bowl down and then placed her arm on his shoulder. "I'm happy too," she said just before kissing him on the cheek. Emma came in with a bowl and quickly turned and left, while Liz pulled over a chair and sat down beside her father. "Things are going to be fine with us now and also when she gets to Columbia just as long as we know that you'll be okay living here by yourself," Liz said to him.

Tom could see that she appeared to be genuinely concerned. "Well, sweetheart, I've thought about that, and what I'm going to do is get more involved at the office. Not that I'm going back to running things 24-7, mind you, but let's just say I'll be doing more than just being the window dressing. At least that will keep my mind active, which is step one. Step two is, I'm going to get more involved with the parish, network locally a lot better than I've done in the past—"

"And perhaps meet someone," Liz cut in.

"Let's not go there just yet, Liz. Your mother still occupies the only place in my heart for that sort of thing—"

"But listen, Daddy, if someone should come along and, say, she looks at you and you look at her—"

"And we get into a staring contest," Tom countered, chuckling a little to himself.

Liz thought it looked like he could possibly be persuaded and decided wouldn't that be better than most of the other alternatives that could be imagined. "Why don't you go onto step three, Daddy? Is there a step three?" Liz asked him.

"Step three, oh yes, there is a step three. If steps one and two fizzle out, I can always sell the house and move down to Florida where my brother Jim lives in one of those active adult places, I think they call them. Your uncle loves it down there, swears he'd never come back north again. But in the meantime—and I don't want to call it step four because I'll never keep track of all these damn steps—but in the meantime, I'm going to do some renovation to the house, shower grab bars, things like that. And I'm going to get a real live housekeeper who can really take care of things around here once your sister is away," Tom said as Emma reentered the room, serving plate in hand.

"What's this I heard about 'once you sister is away'?" Emma asked them as she sat down at the table.

"Oh, Daddy's just giving me his game plan for the fall. He's going to be very self-sufficient," Liz proclaimed.

"That's good news, Father," Emma added, passing the meat plate to him.

"Best-looking hamburgers I've ever seen," he happily said, helping himself with a big smile on his face.

"How are you feeling now, Father?" Emma asked.

Tom took a drink of his soda. "I'm feeling fine. Much better than before. And one thing that I must say is much better than before is the way you two have been, shall I say—"

"The way we have been getting along," Liz interrupted.

"Yes, that's right, the way you two have been getting along. I don't know if you two girls realize it yet just how important it is to a parent, any parent, to see his or her children actually getting along, actually even liking one another. What a novel concept that is," Tom said, laughing to himself.

Liz got up and moved her chair back to its original position. "Well, Father, I have some good news for you on that front. From now on, daughter number one and daughter number two are going to get along just fine together. You wait and see," Liz confidently told him.

"That's wonderful," Tom replied, biting into his burger.

Emma was becoming a bit edgy. She knew she was going to leave the house for Fishkill early the next morning, and it just somehow didn't seem like a good time to break the cover story with all the extra family goodwill in the air.

"Yes, Father," Emma shyly added.

"Come on, Emma, what's bothering you?" Tom asked her.

Emma quickly decided she had better just go through with it. "Well, not to put a damper on things with our family reunion, but I forgot to tell you, Father, that I'll be going out tomorrow with Kate Brown, one of my classmates from Central. We've been planning a Sunday trip into the city—museums, a restaurant, Central Park, and the like. A big getaway, burn-off-some-steam type of day, what with all the stress at school, you know," Emma stumbled as she explained.

Tom laughed, thinking back to his days in college. "Well, it sounds like a great idea. A little too tame for me. When I was in school, boy, can I remember a few things that I won't bother going into at the dinner table. Go ahead, Emma. Get out there and have some fun with your friend. It will do you good," Tom encouraged her.

"Who's Kate Brown?" Liz curiously asked her.

Emma hesitated a moment. "Oh, she's just the girl I see on the bus in the morning. She goes to Central College too, and we walk up the hill together to get to class. She's become a pretty good friend of mine. I like her a lot. She's real smart, and we've hit it off," Emma nervously explained.

173

Liz could see that perhaps there was more to the story than met the eye, but in the interest of all the newfound family togetherness, she decided not to pursue the topic any longer, at least not for the moment.

"So what time will you be leaving, Emma?" Tom asked her, thinking about the potential loss of his home-cooked Sunday morning breakfast. "It'll be early, I think...seven, let's say," Emma answered.

Tom's heart sank a little. "Well, you just go ahead, dear. I'll make breakfast myself tomorrow after I get up at a more reasonable hour for a Sunday," he commented.

"Oh, no need for that, Daddy. I was thinking of staying over, anyway," Liz jumped in, glancing over at her father, who was becoming more preoccupied with his burger. "I'll make you breakfast in the morning, Daddy, before I go back to Columbia. I have most of my things upstairs, and it will be fun having breakfast together again," Liz added, looking back over to her sister.

Tom smiled and then went back to eating. Emma was becoming more nervous. She wanted to sound like everything was all right, but she couldn't find any of the right words to say, so she kept quiet.

"It'll almost be like old times," Liz proclaimed to her father, sensing the nervousness in her sister across the table. Liz's mind flashed to the letter on the bed. She remembered how Emma had acted differently up in her bedroom earlier, and she could see that Emma wasn't exactly comfortable with the idea of her staying over for the night. No, something was rotten in Denmark, as they say, Liz thought to herself. And then it hit her as she tried to figure out in her mind just what exactly was going on before her.

"So tell me, Emma, about this Kate Brown. What type of person is she? What is her personality like? Is she athletic?

Is she studious, serious, laid-back, pushy, motherly? What kind of a girl is she? Tell us, why don't you?" Liz challenged.

Emma's heart began to race. The last part of the question really hit a nerve and then some. "Oh, she's just regular," Emma stuttered while she rose from her chair and retreated into the kitchen.

"What's with her?" Tom asked Liz without thinking much of it.

"Oh, she's probably getting you another hamburger, Father, or something like that," Liz responded, thinking to herself that now she had her answer and that the answer had just been given to her by Emma herself.

The following morning, Emma woke up a little before the others. She looked at the phone on her night table and wondered if she should first make a call to her mother, but then she decided it just wasn't worth it; those long-distance calls showed up on the bill, and this one would probably get noticed.

She got out of bed and washed and dressed in record time and then pulled her bag out of the closet and threw it on the bed. She opened it for a quick check and ran over to her dresser and grabbed the letter on top and stuffed it in the bag. Then she slowly opened her bedroom door and headed over to the staircase and quietly made her way down the stairs. So far, so good, she thought. She went into the kitchen and put down her bag. She pulled out a cheese danish from the refrigerator and put the coffee on. Then she went back to the refrigerator and reached for the eggs but suddenly stopped and looked at her watch and thought the better of it.

Finally, the coffee was ready. She poured, added milk, and gulped down the danish and drank the coffee as fast as she could. Then she quickly rinsed off in the sink and grabbed her bag and quietly headed for the closet near the front door. She thought she heard her father upstairs go into the bathroom. She opened the closet and reached for her coat but then thought the better of it and let go. She turned and ran up the stairs to hear the sound of Tom's electric shaver. Emma opened the bathroom door ever so slightly and called in to her father.

"I'm going now, Daddy. I've got to meet Kate. Have a nice breakfast with Liz," she quickly said.

Tom smiled into the mirror. "Have a wonderful time, dear. And don't do anything I wouldn't do," he quipped, happily laughing at his own joke.

Emma was relieved. She turned and headed back down the stairs for the closet. Emma put her bag down, opened the closet, pulled her coat from the hangar, and put it on. She reached down for her bag, and when she looked up, she saw Liz coming toward her from the stairs.

"I've been up. I didn't sleep so well last night," Liz said to her.

Emma nodded her head. "Not used to the old bed," Emma replied, trying to keep it to small talk. Liz didn't say anything but just watched her. "Well, I'm off," Emma quickly added, reaching for the front door.

"Have a great time," Liz told her, trying to make it seem like everything was normal.

Emma opened the door but then stopped and turned toward Liz. "You have a nice time, too, I mean, having breakfast with Father. Take care of yourself," Emma anxiously remarked, and then she turned and walked out the front door, closing it behind her. Emma got to the sidewalk and took a deep breath, followed by a sigh of relief. She made her way up the street to Forest View Turnpike to her regular morning bus stop. She looked at her watch and saw she was a little behind schedule. Now if only the darn bus would show things could be getting off to a good start, she told herself. She waited several minutes and began feeling like she was under the gun. No bus in sight. It figured, she told herself. She looked at her watch again and this time yelled to herself to just hang in there, that she was still okay with the time.

Then suddenly, as if by some miraculous intervention of the angels, she spotted a yellow cab coming toward her. Excitedly, she stepped out into the street and waved down the old driver. Emma got into the cab and took a deep breath. "Grand Central Station in Manhattan," she told him.

The driver began to pull away slowly. "Lady, there's only one Grand Central Station, and that one Grand Central Station exists only in Manhattan, and you happen to be very lucky today this morning—"

"Yeah, I know. I was able to get a cab," Emma cut in, feeling really good with her newfound sense of freedom.

The old man laughed. "No, you're not lucky for just that reason. You're lucky because it just so happens that I know exactly where it is and how to get there. Most of these young punk drivers today don't know squat," he proclaimed as the vehicle picked up speed heading toward Queens Boulevard.

The driver's rambling on soon died down, and Emma sat back in the seat, imagining what it was going to be like to actually meet her mother. She closed her eyes and pictured a beautiful lady, the same beautiful lady she had seen so often as a child but never got to know, never could be close to. A sense of calming peace came over her as she started up her very own conversation with the beautiful lady inside her mind. A smile appeared on her face as the meditation continued; Emma knew that what she was doing was just plain right.

"That's the Long Island Expressway up ahead. We'll just pop on here, and I'll have you in the city in no time, miss. There won't be much traffic, today being Sunday," the driver said.

"That's great," Emma responded, getting jolted out of her dreamlike trance.

The car drove up onto the ramp, and the driver hit the gas to get onto the expressway's first lane. Emma looked over her shoulder and saw the large shopping mall and the other buildings that lined the boulevard. Funny, she thought to herself, that neither she nor Liz had ever mentioned this place and with all those stores. Oh well, perhaps once the dust settles down, she thought to herself.

A moment passed, and then the image of Liz came back to her, only this time it didn't have anything to do with shopping or shopping centers. Liz looked awfully strange this morning, Emma thought to herself. She certainly seemed to know more than she was spilling, Emma feared as her heart rate and breathing began to increase, just as the entrance to the Queens-Midtown Tunnel came into view.

"Won't be long now, miss," the driver informed her.

"Thank you," Emma answered as he paid the toll.

"So where'd you say you were going again?" the driver asked her, heading into the tunnel.

"I didn't, but I will. I'm headed upstate to a long-awaited family reunion, the kind you read about in books," Emma happily responded to him.

A small smile appeared on the man's face. "Sounds pretty nice, miss. I wish you well. I hope it turns out just the way you must have been dreaming about it in the back seat there," he theorized.

Emma felt a warm, satisfied feeling come over her, as though her belief that she was doing the right thing had just been confirmed. The cab exited the tunnel and got through the lights and made the right turn on Park Avenue and headed north to Grand Central. Emma could feel a jolt of electricity inside her as her first view of the massive station made her new reality seem completely real; her meeting with her mother was actually happening.

The driver pulled up in front of the building and collected the fare. Emma opened the door and started to get out. "Good day to you, miss, and good luck," the old man warmly told her.

"Thanks again, sir," Emma replied and she got out of the car, closed the door, and confidently headed into the terminal. She opened the heavy wood and glass door and walked down the incline into Vanderbilt Hall and then out onto the main space of the station. She looked up at the constellations displayed in the ceiling and then gazed around the enormous expanse until she noticed the large gold clock sitting atop the information center.

"I want to catch the next train to Beacon," she anxiously told the clerk.

"That'll be track forty in twenty minutes," the man replied.

"How much for a round trip ticket?" Emma asked him. "We don't sell tickets here, go over there," the man said, pointing to the other side of the great room where the people were standing on line. Emma thanked him and turned and went over to the slow-moving line for the ticket counter. She finally got to the counter and paid the fare and put her ticket inside her bag. Then she walked over to the numbered tracks. It took a few minutes, but then she found track forty and went midway up the platform and boarded the old diesel train and sat down with the window to her left. Several minutes later, the doors closed, and the train pulled away from the station.

Emma took a deep breath and tried to relax. She leaned back in her seat, shut her eyes, and tried to block out anything that distracted her from seeing her mother in her mind. The train roared through the dark tunnel. The blackness against the window made her feel sleepy, and she began to doze off. Then suddenly, the train emerged from the tunnel into the blinding sunlight, and Emma recoiled and covered her eyes from the stinging rays. After several minutes, she gazed out the window and watched the buildings whizz by. Then she saw what must have been a crew team out on the northern part of East River doing their rowing drills. One of them had a large Columbia banner hoisted up high. Emma smiled at them, but then it made her think of Liz, and she wondered to herself just how much did that sister of hers really know and, more importantly, what she was going to do with it. But no, Emma told herself, this really wasn't the time to allow Liz to ruin her day, to ruin what really amounted to be the biggest day in her life.

"Tickets, please," the gray-haired conductor called out.

Emma turned away from the window and pulled her train ticket out of her bag. "How long to Beacon?" she asked him.

"About fifty-nine minutes, give or take a few," he told her, collecting her ticket and moving away.

The train ride seemed to drag on forever with the view of the Hudson as her only consolation. Finally, the train pulled into Beacon, and Emma grabbed her bag and got off. She looked around and spotted a cab just off the platform next to a phone booth and walked over and got in.

"Where to, miss?" the young man asked.

"I want to go to a private house in Fishkill. The address is 121 Sycamore Road. Do you think you can find it?" Emma asked him.

"No problem. We'll be there in ten minutes, unless we hit a deer crossing, and then it will be eleven," he joked with her.

"I need to make a phone call first. Can you wait here a moment?" she asked.

"No problem," he assured her.

Emma felt relieved exiting the cab and raced over to the phone. She pulled out some coins and tried to gather herself. "Dear God, please make this go well," she prayed, calming her nerves to a slight degree. She then dialed the number that was by now burned into her memory and then nervously waited for her mother to answer. Four rings, five rings… "Come on, answer the damn phone," Emma cried out as her hand began shaking.

"Hello," a woman's voice finally answered.

"Hello, this is Emma. Is this Mary? Mary Hughes?" she sheepishly asked, trembling at what might have been the first sound of her mother's voice.

"Emma, yes, this is Mary. Where are you?" the pleasant-sounding lady inquired.

A tear rolled down the side of Emma's face while she struggled to hold back the emotions welling up inside her. "Can I come over?" Emma asked her.

Mary was delighted. "Certainly. Are you up here, by any chance?" Mary asked her.

"I'm at the station. I have a cab waiting for me," Emma said.

"That's fine. Just tell him to drive carefully, and I'll see you soon," Mary said and then she hung up the phone.

Emma leaped out of the booth and ran back into the cab. "Everything okay?" the driver asked her.

Emma sat back and wiped her eyes. "I'm good to go," she told him, desperately hoping inside her heart that she really was good to go.

The cab made its way along a beautiful scenic road and then turned onto Sycamore. Emma looked out and saw a large expanse of picturesque, rolling farm country. She couldn't help but notice a lack of houses. The cab climbed up a slight hill and turned in at the summit and rolled up on the circular driveway to the impressive house that was set back a few hundred feet. Emma reached into her bag and pulled out the money for the driver.

"Could you please count to twenty before you pull away? Just in case I got the day wrong. You can keep the change," she said to him.

The driver took the money, and a smile lit up across his face. "Thank you very much, and of course. I'll count to thirty if you like," he told her.

Emma got out and walked up onto the porch and rang the front doorbell. A brief moment went by, and then Mary Hughes opened the door. She was a tall, slender, good-looking woman who looked much younger than her actual age. Emma just looked at her for an instant and saw the same eyes, the same stature, the same type of hair, although Mary's was a little on the gray side. It was uncanny.

"Come in, my dear," Mary gently offered, escorting her beyond the large foyer and into the huge living room in the front of the house. "Won't you give me your coat?" Mary asked, also looking Emma over and flashing back in her mind to that time those many years ago.

Emma got out of the coat and handed it to her. Mary tossed it onto the sofa. "Let me look at you, Emma," Mary cautiously said, as though she were almost afraid that the happy event might possibly somehow shatter.

Emma politely smiled. "I'm very happy to see you. I mean, what I mean to say is that I'm just very happy to see you," Emma stumbled, staring into Mary's eyes that bore such an unmistakable resemblance.

"Same here," Mary answered her.

A silent moment went by that seemed much longer to them both. Finally, Mary stepped forward and kissed her on the cheek. "Welcome, and won't you sit down," she suggested, pointing to the sofa.

Emma sat next to her coat. She was feeling somewhat uneasy, somewhat strange from looking at her mother for the first time in this unknown territory.

"Would you like anything to drink?" Mary nervously asked her, feeling the strain of the situation herself.

Emma quietly nodded her head. "Water, please. I'll take some water," she said.

"Okay, one water. Anything else?" Mary encouraged.

Emma didn't know what to say. "No, no thank you. Water. Water will be fine," Emma told her, trying to hide her nerves. Mary turned and left the room to get her drink. Emma let out a large sigh of relief. Then she questioned in her mind how things were going, how she had done. But nothing made sense because her nerves felt like they were almost uncontrollable.

In a moment, Mary returned with a glass and put it on the coffee table in front of Emma. "Let me know if you'd like anything else, and, Emma, let me take a look at you," Mary said with a loving expression on her face. Emma spontaneously jumped up from the sofa. Mary walked over to her and gently put her hand on Emma's shoulder. "My, I can't get over how pretty you are. And what a nice girl you turned out to be too," Mary said in a very tender way.

Emma thought she felt a little of the pressure come off. "Thank you very much, Mary," Emma replied as her eyes welled up a little.

Mary wanted to know more about her. She walked around her to the sofa and sat down and patted the cushion with her hand to get Emma to sit beside her. Emma reached down for the glass and took a drink and then sat down next to her mother.

There was another moment of silence before they both started talking to each other. Mary began to laugh, and the room began to lighten for them both. "What should we do, Emma? What should we talk about? I know. We both have questions we'd like answered, right?" Mary asked.

Emma nodded. "Right," she replied, taking another drink of water.

"Where should we start, Emma? How would you like to start?"

"I'm okay with anything you'd like to do," Emma said.

Mary began to feel vulnerable, as though reliving too much of the past with Emma might not be such a good thing for either one of them. "Well, why don't we do this," Mary nervously suggested. "Why don't we go take a drive, and I'll show you a few things around here. How does that sound?"

Emma wasn't too pleased with the suggestion, but she was afraid to disagree with her, afraid it might set things off to a bad start. "Okay, that sounds good. I'll get my coat on," Emma blurted, leaping back up on her feet.

Mary took the glass and got up and brought it into the kitchen. Then she returned to Emma and pulled her car keys out of her bag. "Do you think I'll need a coat, or will this sweater be enough," Mary asked her, feeling a sense of relief now that she was getting out of the house.

"It's nice out. I think the sweater will be enough," Emma answered. Mary led her to the front door, and they both stepped out onto the porch. "This is really pretty here," Emma complimented her.

"Thank you. It is a pretty place here. Nice and quiet but not so far out into the country that you feel like you're in the middle of nowhere," Mary remarked as she walked over to the late model black Cadillac parked in the driveway. "The doors are open," she called over to Emma, who then got in. Mary started the engine and sat there for a moment, staring out ahead of her. "Where would you like to go? What would you like to see, Emma?" Mary asked.

Emma drew a blank, so Mary continued, "Oh, I've got an idea. We could take a drive over to the club, and I'll show you the golf course if you'd like. It's closed for another week for maintenance, but I think we might be able to just take a ride on the cart path since none of the golfers will be out, or we could go over to the shopping center and have lunch there, or perhaps you'd just like to ride around a little and see the countryside. It's really pretty with the hills and all, or we could—"

"We could go by your club and see the golf course, if that's okay," Emma shyly answered.

"Okay then, the club it is. We can have lunch over there after you get tired of looking at the course, and we can talk about things over there, too, if you like," Mary confidently said now that she was taking charge. She put the car in gear, and they drove out to Sycamore and made a right turn. Mary pointed out toward Emma's window. "We own all of this up to the stone wall coming up on your right in a minute," Mary said. Emma couldn't believe what she was seeing. "It used to belong to my grandfather, then my father, then me. Grandfather used to actually farm it. He was doing pretty good as a farmer too. He planted corn and raised livestock. He even once got the first prize at the fair for a bull he once owned. My father, not so much. He was strictly business— airlines, among other things. He had this thing about airplanes. He always wanted to fly, so he learned how, and then he bought his own airline or commercial air service, however you say it, and he did pretty well. He doubled the company inside of five years and doubled it again over the next ten. So not bad for a guy who just wanted to fly, wouldn't you say?" Mary recounted.

Emma was all ears. "Wow, that's quite interesting, actually. That's quite a family, I mean. I'd really like to hear more about them," Emma continued as Mary pulled up to the entrance of the Willows Country Club and drove past the first parking lot and into the one closest to the clubhouse. She pulled into her reserved space and turned off the motor. A grip of near panic suddenly came over Emma. "Who do you want me to say who I am if anyone comes over to us?" Emma cautiously asked her mother.

Mary thought to herself for a minute. "You're right. I know just about everybody in here. Let's see. You're Emma from St. Theresa's Academy. You are here for a visit. You are friends with…let me see…you are friends with me. Period. That's all they need to know, if that's all right with you," Mary said to her.

"Sounds okay."

"Good. Come on now, I'll show you some of the course, and after we get tired of touring, we'll eat. I'll bet you're starving," Mary said, opening the car door and getting out.

Emma got out and ran up to catch her. "This place is beautiful," Emma quietly said, trying to hold back some of her feelings. They walked toward the main building and then out past the rear of it to the cart shack.

"Hello, Bill, is Jim around? I wanted to know if I could show my young guest some of the course from the cart path, if that's okay. I promise not to drive on the grass," Mary told him.

The young man thought for a moment. "Jim won't be in today, but I guess it'll be all right for you, Ms. Hughes," he answered and then he politely smiled at her and walked away.

Mary reached inside her bag and pulled out another key. "Come on, it's this way," Mary said, leading Emma inside the structure and over to her brand-new golf cart. "We can take it out for a spin. I'll show you some of the course. It's really pretty out there, you'll see," Mary bantered, trying to impress her a little bit. They drove out onto the cart path. Emma could feel the breeze as it blew back her long blond hair.

"Look over there, Emma. That's the second hole, a par three, my first and only—I might add—hole in one. It happened three years ago. I was with Doris, Jane, and Sylvia that day. Doris passed away last year. Anyway, that was my big claim to fame. Poor Doris. It was a terrible car accident. At least she didn't have to suffer, I suppose. Anyhow, do you play golf?" Mary asked her, trying to get off the painful subject.

Emma shook her head. "No, not really. But I've often thought I'd like to. I was a pretty good athlete growing up. I ran track. I even set the record in some of my events. But I gave it up after high school."

"Why'd you give it up?" Mary questioned.

Emma thought back for a moment. "Oh, I don't know. I just did. I guess it just wasn't that important to me anymore. Besides, I wanted to concentrate on my schoolwork when I got to college," Emma explained to her.

Mary's curiosity picked up. "So tell me about your schoolwork, Emma. I like that name. Emma. I think it suits you well," Mary told her.

Emma smiled. "Well, okay, about my schoolwork, well, you see—and I don't want to sound as though I'm bragging—I was very good at math and I was also very good at writing. I used to write a lot as a child. In school back then, I would always enjoy writing compositions. I don't know why but I just did. It just came sort of naturally to me, so whenever we were assigned a topic to write about, well, I just jumped in, and the words came flying out."

"After you did your research first, of course."

"Of course. How did you know that?" Emma asked her.

Mary laughed. "Well, it just so happens that I like to write too. I did well with it in school myself and ended up teaching English, middle-school English, over at the middle school about four miles from our house," Mary fondly recalled. Emma wanted to know more. "Did you ever think of becoming a writer? Novels and things like that?" Emma asked her.

Mary turned to her and smiled. "You read my mind. The answer to your question is yes. I did try my hand at it once. I wrote a novel about a nurse who lost her true love because she had to go out on call too often for his liking, and she, well, you get the picture." Emma chuckled.

"Sounds like it could be a best seller," Emma remarked.

Mary laughed and then shook her head. "Oh yeah, right, best seller my eye. I couldn't get to first base, or should I say, I couldn't get it off the tee, since we were talking about golf a little while ago," Mary bantered, feeling a lot more relaxed with her now.

Emma's mood became somber. "That's too bad. That's too bad about the book and your not being able to get it published. It must have been very frustrating," Emma sympathetically told her.

Mary reached over and grabbed her hand. "It took me a little while, but I got over it. I just went back to my golf game to practice up for that hole in one I told you about," Mary joked as they headed around the bend and up the rise in the cart. Mary pulled over to the right and shut the motor off.

"Take a look out there, Emma. It's the most scenic spot on the course. It's the biggest lake we've got too," Mary said as Emma looked out at the shimmering blue water lying beneath her.

"It's beautiful," Emma raved, being totally captivated by the view.

Mary gave her a moment to soak it all in, and then she looked over right at her. "You know, Emma, I've often wondered just what it might be like, I mean, a moment like this, meeting you and seeing for myself just what you were like, what kind of person you'd grown up to be. And I've got to tell you something. I'm glad I waited and I'm glad I got to see you because all of my wondering couldn't come close to seeing just how wonderful you really are," Mary told her.

Emma blushed a little. The words sounded wonderful to her, almost as if nothing else in the world really mattered, but she also felt at a loss as to how to respond. "Thank you very much, Mary," she quietly said, followed by a moment of them both wondering what to say next. Mary took the lead.

"Well, are you tired of driving around the golf course? Are you getting hungry?" Mary awkwardly asked her. Emma was thrown a bit.

"Well, I'm really not tired of seeing this beautiful place you have here. However, you're right, I am getting hungry. I only threw a small breakfast together before coming up here," Emma replied.

Mary smiled at her. "See, I thought you might be hungry. Come. Let's go over to the dining room and live it up a little," Mary said. She restarted the motor and swung the cart around and headed back toward the club. "So tell me more about your writing, Emma. Are you planning to try for a career in it, or are you thinking about becoming some kind of rocket scientist with your math ability," Mary asked, pushing the cart somewhat faster as she wondered to herself how she might try handling certain questions should they come up.

Emma didn't seem to notice. "Well, to tell you the truth, I'm currently attending Central College, but I'm planning to transfer to Columbia University in the fall, and if things really work out the way I hope, then I'm going to go to law school."

"You mean Columbia's?"

"Yes, that's right. I'm planning for a career in law, just like my father, who is an attorney," Emma hesitated to say.

Mary looked past Emma's nervousness. "Well, I've got to tell you that I'm impressed. I really am. That's terrific. I suppose all that writing ability will come in handy if you're practicing law," Mary pointed out to her as she pulled the golf cart into the cart shack and parked it in its stall. "Come on, Emma. Let's go eat. I know you're hungry," she said, racing out of the building toward the club.

Emma had to hurry to keep up. They entered through the side door and headed down a long corridor and went into the dining room and then over to Mary's usual table.

"You sit there, Emma. That way you can get the view," Mary said as Emma was gazing out at the perfectly manicured golf course. "What do you like to eat? They really have a terrific chef here. I like the salmon myself, but everything is good," Mary said, sitting down and handing her menu to her daughter.

Emma sat and put the menu down. "This place is absolutely breathtaking. The view, the trophies we passed coming in here, the paneled walls, it's simply amazing," Emma stated.

Mary just went right past that. "Come on, I know you're hungry. Why don't you order something that will really break your diet? I mean, with a figure like yours, what's an extra pound or two? Go on, get something good," Mary coaxed her, really enjoying the role of being a mother.

Emma glanced at the menu. A friendly-looking young woman came over to take their order. "Hello, Ms. Hughes, so nice to see you again," the waitress said.

"Kind of empty in here, Katy. I guess they'll all be in a bit later. We're not too early for lunch, are we?" Mary asked.

"I'll speak to the chef, Ms. Hughes. For you, I'm sure there won't be a problem. Will you be having your usual grilled salmon today, Ms. Hughes?" the girl politely asked.

Mary nodded at her. "Yes, Katy, that will be just fine," Mary replied.

"And for you, miss, do you know what you would like, or should I give you another minute?"

Emma quickly reviewed the menu but couldn't really concentrate. "What do you recommend, steak or chicken?" Emma asked her.

The young girl smiled. "Oh, that's an easy one. They really do steak well here. I'd get the filet mignon if I were you. It's really good," the girl told her.

Emma nodded. "Okay, I'll go with the filet, medium, and thank you," Emma politely said as the busboy filled her water glass and then left.

Mary picked up her glass and proposed a toast. "Here's to law school and you becoming a great lawyer," she said, clinking Emma's glass and taking a drink. Emma did the same. "So tell me about the kind of law you're thinking about," Mary asked, trying to find some conversation.

"Probably corporate. That's the type my father practices," Emma let slip out.

Mary was unconcerned. "Is he still practicing?" she asked.

Emma hesitated a minute but then just decided to treat it as normal as possible. "Yes, to answer your question. He is still practicing. He has his own firm and he has done very well. He and my sister, Liz, are both going to be at the firm once she finishes school. She's at Columbia now and will be attending the law school there also," Emma explained.

"Sounds like a plan," Mary said, feeling somewhat sad that the plan didn't include her. "And your sister, Liz, are you two close?" Mary inquired.

Emma's jaw dropped. "Well, you see, Mary, she's a little older, and we do get along, but I can't really say that we are terribly close. It's probably the age thing, but it's okay," Emma revealed.

Mary seemed a little relieved. "So you two do get along."

"Yes," Emma jumped in.

"Well, that's good. I had a sister. Her name was Eileen. She was three years older than me. We did and then we didn't always get along. She thought she was so much smarter. Anyhow, she died a few years ago. She left a husband and two kids, two adult children, I should say," Mary told her.

Emma saw an opening to ask about one of the questions that was worrying her. "What did she die from?" Emma put forth.

Mary was a little surprised. "She had a car hit her while she was crossing the street. The guy ran a red light. It happened over in Beacon. She was over there shopping and then wham, this stupid guy killed her. It was unbelievable," Mary recounted.

Emma paused for a moment. "Well, I guess the reason I'm asking is because I would like to know something, and this story about you having a sister dying, well, I thought it might be from some type of disease, you know, like cancer or something," Emma stated in a roundabout way. Mary couldn't quite see where Emma was heading, so she remained quiet. "I guess what I'm asking is, is there any cancer or heart disease in the family?" Emma finally questioned her.

Mary was fine with it. "I can tell you, Emma, that as far as health issues go, the answer is no. No cancer, no heart disease, just allergies, thank God. Maybe that's why my father wasn't so hot to be a farmer after all," Mary joked with her.

Emma was obviously relieved. "Well, thank you for that. That's good to know," Emma told her just as their lunch was brought over to the table.

"Grilled salmon for you, Ms. Hughes, and for your lovely guest, we have the filet, medium," Katy said, placing the food down before them.

"Looks terrific," Emma commented.

Katy smiled. "I hope you enjoy it. Can I bring you anything else?" Katy asked, turning to Mary.

"I think we're fine, Katy, and please give my thanks to Ralph back in the kitchen," Mary said.

The young waitress smiled and left them. Emma was the first to dig in. She wanted to ask Mary about her father but was simply too afraid. "Could you tell me a little bit about your trip that you mentioned in the letter?" Emma finally asked her.

Mary nodded at her as she cut into her salmon. "I'm going to Ireland for a week this coming Thursday with a group from St. Raymond's, that's my parish. A couple of the girls thought it might be a good idea to see Paris while we were over there rather than just return home from Dublin. Julie Martin and Sylvia Manning have asked me if they could talk me into going with them for my birthday, which will occur when we're in Ireland with the group. I haven't yet decided, but I told them I'd let them know a day or two after we arrived in Ireland," Mary explained.

Emma was really impressed. "That must be something, I mean, to have two friends willing to take you to Paris for your birthday. It must cost a lot," Emma blurted. Mary laughed. Emma felt somewhat embarrassed by her own remark. "When is your birthday?" she quickly asked.

"It's on the sixteenth. Anyhow, back to the story. These two gals are very good friends, very good people, and very wealthy widows. Their husbands left them extremely well off, so to them, the money isn't an issue. They won't even feel it," Mary told her.

Emma didn't know what to say. "Is Sylvia the same one as the Sylvia you shot the hole in one with that day?" Emma asked.

Mary's face brightened as she thought back to that big event. "Same Sylvia, Emma. Yes, that's right," Mary answered.

"So you're not sure when you'll be coming back?" Emma asked, sounding a bit saddened.

Mary could see her reaction. "To tell you the truth, Emma, I just might want to come home from Ireland. There are some business things coming up here for me to keep watch on, and maybe I'll just want to come home. I don't know. The girls will understand, and we can celebrate the birthday in Ireland if need be. Besides, at my age, what's to celebrate?"

"Oh, stop that age business, Mary. You look terrific. And besides, you just got finished telling me we have our board-certified, healthy family," Emma quipped.

Mary was happy to see her talk like that. She looked around the room and saw that the restaurant was empty. "I'm going to tell you one other thing in that regard, Emma. I wasn't married but I knew your father for years, and I can tell you he came from some pretty good healthy stock himself," Mary quietly told her.

"What happened to him, if you don't mind me asking?" Emma said, gathering up her courage.

Mary paused and stared into the distance with a somber look on her face. "He was an army guy. He went to West Point, and when he was commissioned, he got himself into the paratroopers and was stationed in Germany. During a training exercise, his parachute failed to open," Mary revealed, refusing to allow herself to dwell too much on her past sorrow. Emma reached across the table and grabbed hold of her hand and gently squeezed it. "His name was John, Emma. John Penderton," Mary recounted.

Emma squeezed a little tighter. "Thank you for telling me. It was one of the questions I was going to ask, but thank you for my not having to ask it," Emma said, removing her hand from her mother's.

Mary nodded at her and picked up her fork and went back to eating. Emma sat there for a moment looking at her mother, unable to think about anything other than the fact that she felt like she had truly been blessed.

In a few minutes, Katy came back over to the table. "How's everything?" she asked Mary, noticing that they were almost finished eating.

Mary put her fork down and turned to her. "Oh, we're doing just fine. I don't think we'll be having any desert, that is, unless you, Emma—"

"No thank you. I'd be too stuffed," Emma cut in.

"Well, Ms. Hughes, then you two take your time, and I'll just charge it to your account, if you like," Katy said.

"That'll be fine, and add twenty percent for yourself," Mary instructed.

The young waitress smiled and thanked her and then walked away. Mary, too, could see that they were nearly finished. "That was really good. I couldn't eat another thing," Emma remarked.

Mary warmly smiled at her. "What do you think, one or two inches?" she playfully asked.

Emma didn't know what she meant. "One or two inches?" she questioned.

Mary laughed a little to herself. "To your waistline, silly," Mary teased her, getting up from the table. Emma finished her last bite with a grin on her face and got up to join her mother. "Bathroom break is to the right, Emma, if you—"

"No, I'm good," Emma replied as they headed for the exit.

"Hi, Mary," Barbara Tanner called ahead to her before they crossed paths under the exit sign. Barbara was one of those people who knew everything about everybody all the time. Mary felt extremely uncomfortable.

"Barbara, Madeline, how are you two ladies doing? And, Barbara, how is our new golf instructor working out for you?" Mary asked, making polite conversation but wanting to get out of there.

"I went out once with him on the driving range. He seems all right. Say, another week till tee time, huh, Mary," Barbara stated, carefully eyeing Emma up and down.

Mary picked up on her friend's nosiness. "Another week, yes, that's right. This is my young friend Emma from St. Theresa's Academy. Emma has come down to help me with a few things over at the house. A million loose ends before our outing to Ireland, you know how that is," Mary conjured up.

Barbara had a suspicious look on her face. "Yes, Mary, a million loose ends. I don't know how I'll ever be ready for it on time myself," Barbara commented.

Mary saw her opening. "Well, if you ladies will excuse us, I've got a long list awaiting me over at the house, so have a nice day, Barbara, Madeline. And, Barbara, I guess I'll see you Thursday for our big adventure," Mary said, taking hold of Emma's arm and pulling her along with her out the door.

That was close, Emma thought to herself while remaining completely silent. They quickly walked over to Mary's car and got in.

Mary put the key in the ignition but then held up. "What should we two girls do next?" Mary asked with the answer already in mind. Emma wondered to herself about this whole arrangement after the encounter with Barbara, so she kept quiet. Mary turned the key and fired up the engine. "What should we two girls do next? The answer is simple, go shopping," Mary called out with a look of glee in her eye.

Emma quickly glanced at her watch and thought that that might work out nicely for her time-wise. "Like mother, like daughter," Emma carefully said, looking at Mary's face for her reaction.

Mary began to laugh. "I should have known. Shopping. Of course. We can run over to Beacon. They have a few nice shops over there on Main Street. What do you think about that?" Mary asked her.

Emma began to wonder to herself if going back over to Beacon might be part of a plot by her mother to cut the afternoon short. "That sounds pretty good, but aren't there any stores around here we could go to?" Emma asked her, probing her mother for a clue.

Mary pulled the car back and drove out of the lot. "Emma, we don't have too many of what I call good clothing stores in Fishkill or any of the other local villages. Beacon is probably our best bet. Besides, I haven't been over there in a while and I wouldn't mind picking up a few things myself for my trip," Mary casually said.

In Emma's mind, Mary seemed to be acting the same way she did during lunch, so maybe things were actually good with her. She began to feel a little more relieved of her suspicions. "All right, Beacon it is. It should be fine, and hopefully you can fill in for your trip. It sounds like you'll be having a great time over there with your friends," Emma bantered.

Mary pulled out onto the road in a direction that took them away from her house. "I know a shortcut from here with a better view. You'll be able to see some of the really pretty countryside we have up here," Mary remarked as she pulled up to a stop sign and made a right turn into the rolling landscape of small farms and estates. "That house over there is Sylvia's."

"Same Sylvia?" Emma quickly jumped in.

Mary broke out laughing. "Yes, that's right, Emma. The same Sylvia. I never quite thought of her that way before," Mary answered, laughing to herself.

Emma thought she saw an opening, so she worked up her courage. "So how shall I contact you? I mean, when can we get together after your trip with the same Sylvia? And how will I know you got back safely?" Emma asked, almost pleading with her for the right answer.

Mary immediately sensed the urgency. "Oh, Emma, I'm going to be all right. The trip will probably be just to Ireland for me. And you can always call or write," she sympathetically said to her.

Emma wasn't satisfied. "And what if you want or need to call me? How should we work that?" Emma asked.

Mary thought to herself a moment. "Obviously you probably don't want me calling the house—"

"And getting my father, or even worse, my sister," Emma interrupted.

"Right," Mary said with a sigh. A few silent moments passed while they both tried to come up with the answer. "That's Beacon up ahead. Emma, I'm not sure of the best way for me to call you, if need be," Mary remarked.

"Why don't we just go ahead and use a code name or something like that," Emma suggested. "We can be like spies, like we're right out of our own CIA," Emma said, nervously laughing a little to herself.

Mary pulled the car into a space on Main Street. She liked the idea. "Well, what do you know? I just got to see some of that writer's ability of yours. Very good, Emma. We'll be like spies together," Mary said and then she exited the vehicle and walked around onto the sidewalk.

Emma was standing there waiting for her. "Nancy Brown. If you ever need to phone and leave a message, Nancy Brown will be good. It's easy to remember. All you do is drop the name Nancy Brown into any sentence that says anything, and I'll know to call you. How does that sound?" Emma asked.

Mary was impressed. "Well, I think I like that, being in the spy service with you and all," Mary replied, opening the door to a large shop for Emma and herself to go in.

The two women walked inside and began to browse around. Emma wondered just how much damage had Barbara Tanner really done when they left the restaurant, while Mary asked herself just how much talking was that busybody Barbara really going to do. A young sales clerk came over to them and introduced herself.

"Hello, ladies, I'm Jill. Can I help you with anything today? We're having a closeout on some very popular sweaters, if you'd like to see them," she stated.

Mary looked as though she was deep in thought. "I'm really more interested in a light, waterproof jacket. Something you could wear on the golf course," Mary replied.

The girl led them over to the jackets and handed one to Mary to try on. "Not bad, how do I look?" Mary said to Emma.

"It looks really good on you. It should be just what you need for all that Irish rain you always hear about," Emma remarked.

"What do you think? Red, white, or black?" Mary asked.

"Black, definitely black," Emma told her.

"Okay, I'll take it, and could you please show us some sweaters for my friend here," Mary said to the young lady.

"Sure, right over here a little way. We have those closeout sweaters I mentioned," she said, leading them over to the table they were on.

"Very nice. What do you think?" Mary asked, looking right at Emma.

"They're beautiful. I like the gray," Emma remarked. "But I really wasn't going to buy anything."

"Nonsense. My treat. If you don't get one of these to fit, we'll just have to get something else," Mary insisted.

"Would you like to try it on, miss? The dressing room is over there," Jill told her.

Emma took the pullover into the dressing room. A few minutes later, she returned and handed it to the girl. "It fits perfectly—"

"We'll take it," Mary anxiously cut in. "Could you put them in two separate bags?" Mary asked her.

The salesgirl's face lit up. "Right this way. I'll ring you up in no time," she said, leading them over to the register.

A moment later, Mary and Emma were back in the car. "What about your train back?" Mary asked her before starting the engine.

Emma felt like she was being rushed, but she didn't want to show it. "They're running on the hour, every five minutes past the hour," Emma said, only partially able to mask her sadness that it was coming to an end so soon.

"Well, it's five to, and we're about five minutes to the station. What do you say? Should we try to make your train?" Mary coaxed her.

Emma felt a burst of emotion shoot through her. "Will you promise to contact me once you get home from Europe? If I don't hear from you in a little over a week, I'll assume you went to Paris. Promise me. Oh, and just one thing, how much longer would that add to your trip if you do go there to Paris?" Emma asked, sounding a little desperate.

"One extra week," Mary answered. "Then you'll let me know either way once you're home, right?" Emma pleaded.

Mary calmly took hold of her hand and smiled at her. "Emma, of course, don't forget, we're spies together from now on, you and me, remember?" Mary said, trying to console her. Then she started the engine and pulled away from the curb for the station.

Emma was distraught. "So then I can see you again sometime soon after you get back," Emma implored her mother.

Mary became quiet for a moment. She was thinking about Barbara Tanner once more and all the other ones just like her in her world who were just as worrisome, and how she was going to have to deal with the situation. "We'll figure things out after I get back," Mary finally told her. She pulled into the lot and parked next to one of the stairs to the platform and turned the engine off.

Emma felt hurt by what she perceived to be her mother's lack of enthusiasm, but she didn't say a word as she sat there dreading for the train to arrive. Then finally, Emma broke the silence. "Happy birthday, a bit early but happy birthday just the same. And thank you for my sweater," Emma lovingly told her.

Mary sensed a rush of adrenaline come over her as Emma's words made their impact. She felt a strong sense of loss, a loss of time that can never be recaptured but only longed for. A small tear welled up in her right eye. She took a handkerchief out of her bag and wiped it away. Then Mary turned to Emma with a loving look and just stared at her, not really knowing what to say.

Emma leaned over closer to her and kissed her on the cheek and then softly whispered, "I love you," to her mother.

Mary began to tremble as her mind flashed back to that day those many years ago, that day she had last said good-bye to her daughter. Then Mary took hold of Emma's hand. "I love you too," Mary quietly said to her as a sad, almost painful half-smile plainly covered Mary's face. Emma's heart raced. She took a deep breath, exhaled, and then grabbed her two bags and got out of the car and went up the stairs to the platform as the train pulled into the station. The doors opened, and Emma stepped in but then stopped and turned and waved to her mother sitting there in the car. The doors began to close, and Emma ran to the first window seat where she could see the black car so she could wave one more time to her mother before the train left the station. But the black car was already gone. Almost in anguish, Emma slumped down in her seat, and sadly looked at the gray sweater and wondered to herself if she would ever see her mother again.

EPILOGUE

Emma had just awakened when the large black cloud cast its dark shadow over her cozy lounge chair. The seas had become choppy, too rough for her to want to stay out on the cruise ship's deck any longer. She looked at her watch and couldn't believe the time. It seemed like she had just been talking to her old friend, Susan Daniels, moments ago, but that couldn't be right because her watch said that several hours had gone by.

Emma felt a little groggy; she must have dozed off, she thought. The skies were looking more ominous. Not the way they advertised it, Emma thought, looking up at the dark cloud. An older, distinguished-looking steward came over to her.

"Better think about getting inside, miss," he recommended in his authentic English accent.

"What gives with the weather?" Emma asked him with a concerned look on her face.

The old gentleman smiled at her as he held out his hand to help her up from her chair. "Nothing to get nervous about, miss. Just one of them big blows we run into now and again. But you had better head in just to be on the safe side. Would you like me to escort you, or would you prefer to go in by yourself?" he politely asked her.

Emma smiled at him and then reached down and picked up her bag. "No, no thank you. I'll go in by myself, sir…"

"John. The name is John, miss, and thank-you. But please see to it you do. If it kicks up any more it could get dangerous. I don't want anything happening to you, now, do I? Do you know what me mother use to say? She always said that no matter how bad things got, life was always worth living. Good-day to you, miss. I'll go and continue on me rounds then," he said, and he walked away. Emma went over and stood alone by the rail and closed her eyes. "Thank-you, Mother, for giving me my life, for letting me come into the world when it must have been very difficult for you to do so," she said out loud. The ship rolled a bit, forcing her to grab onto the horizontal structure. Emma then began to walk toward the door up ahead. But she suddenly stopped, and grabbed onto the rail again. She looked out over the dark water and saw her mother sitting in the car at the Beacon train station, those many years ago. She began to cry, remembering the gray sweater, and feeling an even greater sense of loss than she had felt that day. She turned and looked down the length of the empty deck. She saw a woman walking toward her in the distance. The woman kept coming; it looked like Susan Daniels. Emma's heart raced. She couldn't bear to have to deal with her curious friend. Finally, the woman turned in at the entrance to The Admiral's Cove.

Emma turned back and faced the dark ocean. "I'll never give up. I won't let them beat me," she told her mother, more determined than ever to never relive what came after her train ride home from Beacon.

THE END.

About
The Author

Robert Oberle was raised in Queens, New York. He attended school there and went on to graduate from St. John's University with a bachelor's degree in Business Administration. While at St. John's, he was fortunate to be selected into a new program for writers. After graduating, Robert had a career in real estate appraisal in banking, while living in both New York and Thousand Oaks, California. He and his wife, Lynn, eventually returned to the New York Metro area where they currently live. Robert is now writing novels that he feels are interesting and enriching for his readers.

Printed in the USA
CPSIA information can be obtained
at www.ICGtesting.com
JSHW080738160823
46612JS00001B/75